Praise for Walter Tevis

"Entertainment of a high order. . . . Tevis makes you care about his quirky characters. . . . Tevis wrote like a dream, and he told some wonderful stories."

—*Los Angeles Times*

"[Tevis is] a master manipulator of archetypes, an artist capable of delving into the zeitgeist while nevertheless remaining on his own pure search for himself."

—Jonathan Lethem

"[Tevis's] work is unique, with that element of infinite rereadability Nabokov held the hallmark of great literature. Like his characters . . . Tevis's work will endure."

—*Fantasy & Science Fiction*

"More than a one-hit wonder. . . . [Tevis's] writing is invariably clear, his prose tautly built."

—*The Washington Post*

"Tevis has a gift for vivid characterization and propulsive narrative. . . . His style is direct and efficient, never calling attention to itself; yet it grows in power through the course of a novel by its very naturalness."

—Tobias Wolff

"With intense grace, Tevis finds the art to describe art."
—*The Village Voice*

"Tevis's characters, no matter how fantastic or far-fetched, whether they are gamblers or aliens, always feel true. At times, reality has even bent toward his fictions, rather than the other way around. . . . His fiction feels as true as ever." —The Ringer

Walter Tevis

THE HUSTLER

Walter Tevis is the author of *The Hustler*, *The Man Who Fell to Earth*, *Mockingbird*, *The Steps of the Sun*, *The Queen's Gambit*, *The Color of Money*, and the short story collection *Far from Home*. *The Hustler*, *The Man Who Fell to Earth*, and *The Color of Money* were all adapted for film. *The Queen's Gambit* was the basis for the Emmy-nominated Netflix series, and *The Man Who Fell to Earth* is the basis of the Showtime series. Tevis died in 1984.

www.waltertevis.org

Also by Walter Tevis

The Man Who Fell to Earth

Mockingbird

The Steps of the Sun

The Queen's Gambit

The Color of Money

Far from Home

THE HUSTLER

THE HUSTLER

Walter Tevis

Vintage Books
A Division of Penguin Random House LLC
New York

FIRST VINTAGE BOOKS EDITION, JANUARY 2022

The Library of Congress has cataloged the Harper edition as follows:
Name: Tevis, Walter S.
Title: The hustler.
Description: First edition. | New York : Harper, 1959.
Identifiers: LCCN 58013814
Subjects: LCSH: Pool (Game)—Fiction.
Classification: LCC PZ4.T342 PS3570.E95 (print)
LC record available at https://lccn.loc.gov/58013814

Vintage Books Trade Paperback ISBN: 978-0-593-46750-3

Book design by Nicholas Alguire

www.vintagebooks.com

Printed in the United States of America
10 9 8 7 6 5 4 3 2 1

THE HUSTLER

1

HENRY, black and stooped, unlocked the door with a key on a large metal ring. He had just come up in the elevator. It was nine o'clock in the morning. The door was a massive thing, a great ornate slab of oak, stained once to look like mahogany, ebony now from sixty years of smoke and dirt. He pushed the door open, shoved the door stop in place with his lame foot, and limped in.

There was no need to turn the lights on, for in the morning the three huge windows along the side wall faced the rising sun. Outside of them was much daylight, much of downtown Chicago. Henry pulled the cord that parted the heavy draperies and these gathered in grimy elegance to the edges of the windows. Outside was a panorama of gray buildings; between them, patches of a virginal blue sky. Then he opened the windows, a few inches from the bottom. Air puffed abruptly and small eddies of dust and the aftermaths of four-hour-old cigarette smoke whirled and then began to dissipate. Always by afternoon the draperies would be drawn tight, the windows shut; only in the morning was the tobaccoed air exchanged for fresh.

A poolroom in the morning is a strange place. It has stages; a daily metamorphosis, a shedding of patterned skins. Now, at 9 A.M., it could have been a large church, still, sun coming through stained windows, wrapped into itself, the great tables' timeless and massive mahogany, their green cloths discreetly hidden by gray oilcloth covers. The fat brass spittoons were lined along both walls between the tall chairs with seats of honest and enduring leather, rump-polished to an antique gloss, and, above all, the high, arched ceiling with its four great chandeliers and its many-paned skylight—for this was the top floor of an ancient and venerable building which, squat and ugly, sat in eight-story insignificance in downtown Chicago. The huge room, with the viewers' chairs, high-backed, grouped reverently around each of the twenty-two tables, could have been a sanctuary, a shabby cathedral.

But later, when the rack boys and the cashier came in, when the overhead fans were turned on and when Gordon, the manager, would play music on his radio, then the room would adopt the quality that is peculiar to the daytime life of those places which are only genuinely alive at night—the mid-morning quality of night clubs, of bars, and of poolrooms everywhere—the big, nearly empty room echoing the shuffling of a few feet, the occasional clinking of glass or of metal, the sounds of brooms, of wet rags, of pieces of furniture being moved around, and the half-real music that comes from radios. And, above all, the sense of the place's not yet being alive, yet having now within it the first beginnings of the evening resurrection.

And then, in the afternoon, when the players began to come in in earnest, and the tobacco smoke and the sounds of hard, glossy balls hitting one another and the squeaking sound of chalk squares pressed against hard leather cue tips would begin, then would start the final stage of the metamorphosis ascending to the full only when, late at night, the casual players and the drunks would all be gone, leaving only the intent men and the furtive, who watched and bet, while certain others—a small, assorted coterie of men, both drably dressed, who all knew one another but seldom spoke—played quiet games of intense and brilliant pool on the tables in the back of the room. At such times this poolroom, Bennington's, would be alive in a distinct way.

Henry took a broad broom from a closet near the door and began, limping, to sweep the floor. Before he had finished, the cashier came in, turned on his little plastic radio, and began counting out money into the cash register. The bell on the register rang out very loudly when he punched the key that opened it. A voice on the radio wished everyone a good morning.

Henry finished the floor, put the broom away, and began taking the covers from the tables, exposing the bright green baize, now dirty with streaks of blue chalk and, on tables where the salesmen and office clerks had played the night before, smeared with white talcum powder. After folding the cover from each table and placing it on a shelf in the closet, he took a brush and rubbed the wooden rails with it until they glowed with a warm brown. Then he brushed the cloth until the chalk and powder marks and dirt were gone and the green was bright.

2

EARLY IN THE AFTERNOON, a tall heavy man wearing green suspenders over his sport shirt was practicing on the front table. He was smoking a cigar. This he did in a manner like that with which he practiced, thoughtfully and with restraint. A patient man, he would mouth the cigar slowly, with the even, gentle mastication of a cow, reducing the end of it by stages to whatever state of moist deformation pleased his fancy. He played his practice shot patiently, always at the same speed, always in the same pocket, and—almost always—making it fall into the pocket gently and firmly. It seemed neither to please nor displease him to make the ball; he had been shooting this shot, for practice, for twenty years.

A younger man, with a lean ascetic face, was watching him. This man was dressed, although it was summer, in a black suit. He wore a perpetually distraught expression, and often would wring his hands as if in grief, or nervously snuff his nose with his forefinger. On some afternoons, his look of anxiety would be heightened by a strained expression in his eyes and a dilation of the pupils. At such times, however, he would not snuff his nose but would, instead, occasionally giggle to himself. Those were the times when he had been lucky with the games the night before and had been able to buy cocaine. He was not a pool player himself but earned a slender living from making side bets whenever possible. He was known as the Preacher.

After some time, he spoke, snuffing his nose to quiet the voice of his monkey, the insistent whispering of his drug habit, which was beginning to whine. "Big John," he said to the man practicing, "I got news, I think."

The big man finished his stroking of the ball, the steady motion of his fleshy arm undisturbed by the interruption. He watched the bright three ball roll up the table, against the rail, and ease its way back down and into the corner pocket. Then he turned, looked at the Preacher, removed his cigar, contemplated it, looked back at the Preacher, and said, "You think you got news? What does that mean, you *think* you got news?"

Cowed by this, the Preacher seemed confused. "I heard . . . They said, last night, over at Rudolph's house. There was this guy in the game, playing draw, and he said he just come up from Hot Springs at the races. . . ." The Preacher's voice had become stringy. Upset by Big John, his monkey's whine was becoming scratchy. He rubbed his forefinger under his nose, hard. ". . . he said Eddie Felson was there, in Hot Springs, and he said he was coming up here. Maybe tomorrow he's coming, Big John."

Big John had long since mouthed his cigar again. He removed it once more and looked at it. It was very soft. This seemed to please him, for he smiled. "Fast Eddie?" he said, raising his massive eyebrows.

"That's what he said. He was dealing the cards out and he said, 'I saw Fast Eddie Felson down in Hot Springs and he told me he might be coming up this way. After the races.'" The Preacher rubbed his nose. "He said Eddie didn't do so good in Hot Springs."

"I hear he's pretty good," Big John said.

"They say he's the best. They say he's got a real talent. Guys who seen him play say he's the best there is."

"I heard that before. I heard that before about a lot of second-rate hustlers."

"Sure." The Preacher transferred his attention to his ear, which he began pulling, speculatively, as if trying feebly to appear intelligent. "But everybody says he pushed over Johnny Varges out in L.A. Pushed him over flat." Pulling the ear, and then for emphasis—for Big John was, again, impassive—"Like piss on the highway. Flat."

"Johnny Varges could have been drunk. Did you see the game?"

"No, but . . ."

"Who did?" Suddenly Big John seemed to come to life. He jerked the cigar from his mouth and bent down toward the Preacher, staring at him hard, "You *ever* see anybody who *ever* saw Fast Eddie Felson shoot pool?"

The Preacher's eyes darted back and forth, as if looking for a hole where he could hide. Seeing none, he said, "Well . . ."

"Well, what?" Big John kept staring at him, hard, not blinking.

"Well, no."

"No. Hell, no." Straightened up, Big John threw his arms out, invoking the Almighty. "And who, in the name of holy God, has ever *once* seen this man? I ask you. Nobody. That's my answer. Nobody." He turned to the table and took his three ball from the corner pocket, setting it on the green. Then he began chalking his tip, deliberately, as if he were now through with the conversation, the matter settled.

It took the Preacher a minute to regain his composure, to gather his tortured wits. Finally, he said, "But you heard Abie Feinman, what he said they was saying about Fast Eddie out West, about him and Texaco Kid and Varges and Billy Curtiss and all them others he's took. And this guy over Rudolph's house last night he said they don't talk nothing else in Hot Springs these days but Fast Eddie Felson."

"So?" Big John left his three ball, turned scornfully, took his cigar from his mouth. "So did this big man from Hot Springs see Eddie shoot pool?"

"Well, you see . . . It seems this guy he runs some kind of large con game with the races—I think maybe he plays the inside on a traveling wire game—and he says he was kind of busy with his customers. But he says . . ."

"Okay. Okay, I heard it. You told me." Big John turned back to his shot, stroked his cue. The ball rolled, bounced, plopped in the corner pocket. He set it up again. Plop. Again.

The Preacher watched him, silently, wondering when he would miss. Big John kept shooting the three ball, up and down the table, into the pocket. Each time the ball hit the pocket the Preacher snuffed his nose. Then, finally, the ball came down the table an almost imperceptible fraction of an inch closer to the rail than normally. It caught the corner of the pocket, oscillated a moment, then became still. Big John picked up the ball, held it in his heavy right hand and glared at it, not with scorn but with disapproval—he had missed the shot many times before, in twenty years. Then he dropped it firmly into the pocket, turned back to the Preacher and said, "And who is he, this Fast Eddie? Six months ago whoever heard of Fast Eddie?"

The Preacher was startled for a moment. "How's that?" he said.

"So everybody talks Fast Eddie. So who is he?"

The Preacher pulled at his ear. "Well . . . this guy I was telling you about says he used to hustle out on the Coast. California. Says he just come on the road, maybe two, three months ago. Never played Chicago yet."

Big John took his cigar from his mouth, looked at it with displeasure, threw it, gently, into a brass cuspidor that was on the floor, beneath the powder holder. It hissed when it hit, and both of them watched the cuspidor for a moment as if waiting for something to happen. When nothing did, Big John turned his stare back to the Preacher. Cigar and three ball now gone, his concentration was complete. The Preacher seemed visibly to wither before its intensity.

"Thirty years ago," Big John said, "*I* was a big reputation. Like Fast Eddie. I had a talent. Thirty years ago I wore hip boots and lived in Columbus, Ohio, and rode to the poolroom in a *taxi*—a *taxicab*—and I played the boys who came in from the factories and I played the little big-time boys from the sticks and, by God, I smoked twenty-five cent cigars. And, by God, I came to Chicago." He stopped for breath a moment, but did not lessen the intensity of his stare. "I came to this great big goddamned city and I was a big reputation. They whispered about me the first time I ever set foot in this poolroom and they put the finger on me for Big John from Columbus and they steered me to old Bennington himself, the man whose name was right on the sign outside the door of this godforsaken poolroom just like it is now except it was on wood and not on neon. And I was hot, good Lord, I was a red-hot pool player from Columbus, Ohio, a big man from out of town. And you know what happened to me when I played Bennington, the man himself, on table number three," he pointed at it, a sturdy, enduring mahogany pool table, "that table right there, for twenty dollars a game? Do you know what happened?"

The Preacher shifted his weight uneasily. "Well. Maybe I do. I think so. . . ."

Big John threw his hands in the air. He was like a colossus. "You *think* so. Good Lord, man, don't you *know* nothing?"

Somehow, the Preacher allowed himself to show a bit of resentment in the center of all the fury that was being focused on him. "Okay," he said, "you lost. I guess he beat you."

Big John seemed to approve of this. He brought his tremendous hands back down, placed them firmly on his hips and leaned forward. "Preacher," he said, softly, "I got my big fat ass beat. Just beat right off."

He remained silent for a minute. The Preacher looked at the floor. Then Big John went back to the table, picked the three ball from the pocket, and held it in his hand, speculatively.

Finally, the Preacher looked up and said, "But you're still a hustler. Hell, you're one of the best in town, Big John. And, besides, that don't mean Fast Eddie . . ."

"The hell it don't. Since I walked in that door over there thirty years ago I never heard nothing but talk about big men coming in from out of town. I've had big boys come in from Hot Springs and Atlantic City and take me for my whole pocket. But I never was a top hustler and never will be. And they don't—they don't never—come in from Mississippi or Texas or California and play heads up with a top Chicago hustler and walk out with more on the hip than they walked in with. It don't happen. It don't never happen."

The Preacher snuffed his nose. "Hell, Big John," he said, "maybe every now and then somebody's bound to . . . Hell, you know how pool is."

Big John jerked a virgin cigar from his shirt pocket. "I know how pool is?" he said. "*I* know how pool is?" He tore the wrapper from the cigar, balled the cellophane up in his hand. "My God, I tried to tell you. I tried to tell you I know this game of pool and I tried to tell you nobody," he bent forward, "*no-bo-dy* ever comes in here and beats George the Fairy or Jackie French or Minnesota Fats. Not heads up, not when he picks up a stick and they pick up a stick and Woody or Gordon racks the balls and they play any game of pool you or me or Willie Hoppe can ever with the help of the Holy Lord name, guess or invent. If somebody gives out handicaps, or if George the Fairy or Jackie French starts spotting balls maybe it's a two-way game of pool. But no hotshot from Columbus, Ohio, or from California is going to beat a top Chicago hustler." He jammed the cigar in his mouth, not even pausing to moisten it beforehand. "So *now* what about Fast Eddie Felson," he said, "from California?"

The Preacher snuffed his nose. "Okay," he said, "okay. I'll wait till he gets here." And then, almost inaudibly, "But he flattened out Johnny Varges. Maybe it was Hot Springs, but he flattened him out."

Big John seemed not to hear this. He had been holding his three ball all of this time and he set it, now, back on its spot on the table. He set the cue ball behind it. He began chalking his cue. Then he said, quietly now, "We'll see how he makes out with Minnesota Fats." He shot the three ball, gently, and it followed its little pattern of motion, its orbit, across the green, into the corner pocket. Then he reached in his own pocket, pulled out a loose and crumpled dollar bill, and laid it on the rail. "Go buy yourself some dope," he said. "I'm tired of watching you rub your damn nose."

3

AT ABOUT THIS TIME two men walked into The Smoker: Pool Hall, Stag Bar, and Grill, in Watkins, Illinois. They seemed to be road weary; both were perspiring although they both wore open-collar sport shirts. They sat at the bar and the younger man—a good-looking, dark-haired fellow—ordered whiskey for them. His voice and manners were very pleasant. He asked for bourbon. The place was quiet, empty except for the bartender and for a young Negro in tight blue jeans who was sweeping the floor.

When they got their drinks the younger man paid the man behind the bar with a twenty-dollar bill, grinned at him and said, "Hot, isn't it?" Now this grin was extraordinary. It did not seem right for him to grin like that; for, although pleasant, he was a tense-looking man, the kind who seems to be wound up very tightly; and his dark eyes were brilliant and serious, almost childishly so. But the grin was broad and relaxed and, paradoxically, natural.

"Yeah," the bartender said. "Someday I'm getting a air conditioner." He got the man his change, and then said, "You boys just passing through, I guess?"

The young man grinned the extraordinary grin again, over the top of his drink. "That's right." He looked to be no more than twenty-five. A nice-looking kid, quietly dressed, pleasant, with bright, serious eyes.

"Chicago?"

"Yes." He set the glass down, only half empty, and began sipping from the water glass, glancing with apparent interest toward the group of four pool tables that filled two-thirds of the room.

The bartender was not normally a garrulous man; but he liked the young fellow. He seemed sharp; but there was something very forthright about him. "Going or coming out?" the bartender said.

"Going in. Got to be there tomorrow," he grinned again. "Sales convention."

"Well, you boys got plenty of time. You can drive in in two, maybe three, hours."

"Say, that's right," the younger man said, pleasantly. Then he looked at his companion. "Come on, Charlie," he said, "let's shoot some pool. Wait out the heat."

Charlie, a balding, chubby-looking little man with the appearance of a straight-faced comedian, shook his head. "Hell, Eddie," he said, "you know you can't beat me."

The younger man laughed. "Okay," he said, "I got ten big

dollars says I beat your ass." He fished a ten from his stack of change in front of him on the bar, and held it up, challengingly, grinning.

The other man shook his head, as if very sadly. "Eddie," he said, easing himself up from the bar stool, "it's gonna cost you money. It always does." He pulled a leather cigarette case from his pocket and flipped it open with a stubby, agile thumb. Then he winked gravely at the bartender. "It's a good thing he can afford it," he said, his voice raspy, dry. "Seventeen thousand bucks' worth of druggist's supplies he's sold last month. Fastest boy in our territory. Getting an award at the convention, first thing tomorrow."

The young man, Eddie, had gone to the first of the four tables and was taking the wooden rack from the triangle of colored balls. "Grab a stick, Charlie," he called, his voice light. "Quit stalling."

Charlie waddled over, his face still completely without expression, and took a cue from the rack. It was, as Eddie's had been, a lightweight cue, seventeen ounces. The bartender was something of a player himself, and he noticed these choices. Pool players who know better use heavy cues, invariably.

Eddie broke the balls. When he shot he held the cue stick firmly at the butt with his right hand. The circle of finger and thumb that made his bridge was tight and awkward. His stroke was jerky, and he swooped into the cue ball fiercely, as if trying to stab it. The cue ball hit the rack awry, much of the energy of the break shot was dissipated, the balls did not spread wide. He looked at the spread, grinned at Charlie, and said, "Shoot."

Charlie's game was not much better. He showed all of the signs of being a fair-to-middling player; but he had much of

Eddie's awkwardness with the bridge, and the appearance of not knowing exactly what to do with his feet when he stepped up to shoot. He would keep adjusting them, as if he were unstable. He stroked very hard, too; but he made a few decent shots. The bartender noticed all of this. Also he watched the exchange of money after each game. Charlie won three in a row, and after each game the two of them had another drink and Eddie gave Charlie a ten-dollar bill from a wallet that bulged.

The game they were playing was rotation pool, also called sixty-one. Also called Boston. Also—mistakenly—called straights. The most widely played pool game of them all, the big favorite of college boys and salesmen. Almost exclusively an amateur's game. There are a few men who play it professionally, but only a few. Nine ball, bank, straight pool, one-pocket are the hustler's games. Any of them is a mortal lock for a smart hustler, while there is too much blind luck in rotation. Except when the best hustlers play it.

But this last was beyond the bartender's scope. He knew the game only as another favorite of amateurs. The serious players around his place were nine-ball men. Why, he had seen one of the players who lived in town run four straight games of nine ball, once, without missing a shot.

The bartender kept watching, interested in the game—for in a small-town poolroom, a ten-dollar bet is a large one—and eventually a few of the town regulars began to drift in. Then after a while the two men were playing for twenty and it was getting late in the afternoon and they were still drinking another one after each game or so and the younger man was getting drunk. And lucky. Or getting hot or getting with it. He was beginning to win, and he was high and strutting, beginning to jeer at the other man in earnest. A crowd had formed around the table, watching.

And then, at the end of the game, the fourteen ball was in a difficult position on the table. Three or four inches from the side rail, between two pockets, it lay with the cue ball almost directly across from it and about two feet away. Eddie stepped up to the shot, drew back, and fired. Now what he obviously should have done was to bank the fourteen ball off the side rail, across the table and into the corner pocket. But instead, his cue ball hit the rail first, and, with just enough English on it to slip behind the colored ball, caught the fourteen squarely and drove it into the corner pocket.

Eddie slammed his cue butt on the floor, jubilantly, turned to Charlie, and said, "Pay me, sucker."

When Charlie handed him the twenty, he said, "You ought to take up crapshooting, Eddie."

Eddie grinned at him. "What do you mean by that?"

"You know what I mean. You were trying to bank that ball." He turned his face away, "And you're so damn blind pig lucky you got to make it coming off the rail."

Eddie's smile disappeared. His face took on an alcoholic frown. "Now wait a minute, Charlie," he said, an edge in his voice, "Now wait a minute." The bartender leaned against the bar, absorbed.

"What do you mean, wait? Rack the balls." Charlie started pulling balls out of the pockets, spinning them down to the foot of the table.

Eddie, suddenly, grabbed his arm, stopping him. He started

putting the balls back in the pockets. Then he took the fourteen ball and the cue ball and set them on the table in front of Charlie. "All right," he said. "All right, Charlie. Set 'em up the way they were."

Charlie blinked at him. "Why?"

"Set 'em up," Eddie said. "Put 'em like they were. I'm gonna bet you twenty bucks I can make that shot just like I made it before."

Charlie blinked again. "Don't be stupid, Eddie," he said, gravely. "You're drunk. There's nobody gonna make that shot and you know it. Let's play pool."

Eddie looked at him coldly. He started setting the balls on the table in approximately the same positions as before. Then he looked around him at the crowd, which was very attentive. "How's that?" he said, his voice very serious, his face showing drunken concern. "Is it right?"

There was a general shrugging of shoulders. Then a couple of noncommittal "I guess so's." Eddie looked at Charlie. "How is it by you? Is it okay, Charlie?"

Charlie's voice was completely dry. "Sure, it's okay."

"You gonna bet me twenty dollars?"

Charlie shrugged. "It's your money."

"You gonna bet?"

"Yes. Shoot."

Eddie seemed greatly pleased. "Okay," he said. "Watch." He started chalking his cue, overcarefully. Then he went to the talcum powder holder and noisily pumped a great deal too much powder into his hands. He worked this up into a dusty white cloud, wiped his hands on the seat of his pants, came back to the table, picked up his cue, sighted down it, sighted at the shot, bent down, stroked, stood up, sighted down his cue, bent down again, stroked the ball, and missed.

"Son of a bitch," he said.

Somebody in the crowd laughed.

"All right," Eddie said. "Set 'em up again." He pulled a twenty out of his billfold and then, ostentatiously, set the still bulging wallet on the rail of the table.

"Okay, Charlie," he said, "set it up."

Charlie walked over to the rack and put his cue stick away. Then he said, "Eddie, you're drunk. I'm not gonna bet you any more." He began rolling down his sleeves, buttoning the cuffs. "Let's get back on the road. We gotta be at that convention in the morning."

"In the morning's ass. I'm gonna bet you again. My money's still on the table."

Charlie didn't even look at him. "I don't want it," he said.

At this moment another voice broke in. It was the bartender from behind the bar. "I'll try you," he said, softly.

Eddie whirled, his eyes wide. Then he grinned, savagely. "Well," he said. "Well, now."

"Don't be a sap," Charlie said. "Don't bet any more money on that damn fool shot, Eddie. Nobody's gonna make that shot."

Eddie was still staring at the bartender. "Well, now," he said, again, "so you want in? Okay. It was just a friendly little bet, but now you want in it?"

"That's right," the bartender said.

"So you figure I'm drunk and you figure I'm loaded on the hip so you want to get in, real friendly, while all the money's still floating." Eddie looked over the crowd and saw, instantly, that they were on his side. That was very important. Then he said, "Okay, I'll let you in. So first you set up the shot." He set thc two balls on the table. "Come on. Set it up."

"All right." The bartender came out and placed the two balls on the table, with some care. Their position was, if anything, more difficult than it had been.

Eddie's billfold was still on the rail. He picked it up. "Okay," he said, "you wanted to get some easy money." He began counting out bills, tens and twenties, counting them onto the middle of the table. "Look," he said, "here's two hundred dollars. That's a week's commission and expenses." He looked at the bartender, grinning, "You bet me two hundred dollars and you get a chance at your easy money. How about?"

The bartender tried to look calm. He glanced around him at the crowd. They were all watching him. Then he thought about the drinks he had served Eddie. It must have been at least five. This thought comforted him. He thought, too, about the games he had watched the men play. This reassured him.

And the young man had an honest face. "I'll get it out of the till," the bartender said.

In a minute he had it, and there were four hundred dollars in bills out on the table, down at the end where they wouldn't affect the shot. Eddie went to the powder dispenser again. Then he got down, sighted, took aim awkwardly, and stroked into the cue ball. Now there was only the slightest difference between that stroke and the stroke he had used all evening—a slight, imperceptible regularity, smoothness, to the motion. But only one man present noticed this. That man was Charlie; and when every other set of eyes in the poolroom was focused in silent attention on the cue ball, an amazing thing happened to the set features on his round face. He smiled, gently and quietly—as a father might smile, watching a talented son.

The cue ball came off the rail and hit the fourteen with a little click. The fourteen ball rolled smoothly across the table and fell softly into the corner pocket. . . .

4

WHEN THEY GOT IN THE CAR Eddie was whistling softly between his teeth. He threw his coat, gaily, in the back seat, slipped behind the wheel, and started fishing the crumpled bills, mostly fives and tens, from his pants pockets. He smoothed them out on his knee, one at a time, counting them aloud as he did so.

Charlie's face and voice were, as ever, expressionless. "Look," he said, "it's two hundred profit and you know it. So let's drive."

Eddie gave him an especially broad grin. He enjoyed doing this, knowing that the charm had no measurable effect on Charlie. "So who's in a hurry," he said, enjoying the simple pleasure of victory. "This is how I get my kicks. Counting the paper."

The car was an incredibly dusty Packard sedan of middle age. After tiring of the money Eddie folded the bills neatly, slipped the roll into his pocket, and started the engine. "That poor guy behind the bar," he said, grinning. "He's gonna have a time explaining to the boss where that deuce went."

"He asked for it," Charlie said.

"Sure. We all ask for it, everybody. We all oughtta be goddamn glad we don't get it too."

"He was greedy," Charlie said. "I could see when we walked in he was the greedy type."

They drove along the highway for about an hour, silently except for Eddie's whistling through his teeth. He played the radio for a while, listened to some very bad music, was admonished to drink Mogen David wine, drive safely over the weekend, drink Royal Crown Cola (best by taste test) and buy bonds. After this last hustle Eddie flipped the radio off and said, "So how're we doing?"

Charlie fished out his cigarette case and automatically pulled out a cigarette for Eddie before lighting his own. Then he said, "You got about six thousand now."

Eddie seemed pleased with this, although he, of course, already knew where they stood. "That's pretty good," he said, "for a beginner. Four months out of Oakland; six thousand. And," he laughed, "expenses. Hell," he lit his cigarette with one hand, the other holding the wheel, "if I hadn't of been a damn fool and dropped that eight hundred in Hot Springs we'd have seven thousand. I should of let that guy quit, Charlie, like you told me. I can't give every hot shot I come heads up with two balls in a bank pool game."

"That's right." Charlie lit his own cigarette.

Eddie laughed. "Well, live and learn," he said. "I'm pretty good, but I ain't that good." Abruptly, he rammed the accelerator, cut the wheel and began shooting past a line of cars they had been dawdling behind for maybe ten minutes. Passing the fourth car he spotted a truck approaching and brake-squealed back into line.

"You aren't that good either," Charlie said, and Eddie laughed again.

"This car's all right," he said, grinning. "It plays a pretty tough game. And you know what, Charlie? After we finish up, after I get, say, fifteen thousand and enough money to fly back home, I'm gonna give you this car."

"Thanks," Charlie said, with gravity, "and ten per cent."

"And ten per cent." He laughed and cut back out into the passing lane. The old Packard, with surprising determination, shot past the rest of the line of traffic. Back in the driving lane Eddie settled it down to a steady seventy miles an hour.

After a minute Charlie spoke again. "What's the hurry?"

"I want to get there. To Bennington's." He paused. "This is gonna be the part that counts. I been wanting to see Bennington's place for a long time."

Charlie seemed to think about this for a minute. Then he said, "Look, Eddie. Remember I asked you to stay out of Chicago? Altogether."

Eddie tried to keep the annoyance from showing. He let the words sit a moment, then he said, "Why?"

Charlie's voice was flat as ever. "You might get beat."

Eddie kept his eyes on the road. "So maybe I shouldn't gamble in the first place, I might get beat. Maybe I should be a salesman. Drugs, maybe."

Charlie flipped his cigarette butt out of the window. "Maybe you are."

"What does that mean?"

"It means you're the kind of pool hustler sells a bill of goods. The kind of high-class con man every mark gets friendly with. First time you ever walked into my place back home you weren't sixteen years old and you were selling a bill of goods."

Eddie grinned. "So I know how to set up a good game for myself, so what? Is that bad?"

"Look, Eddie, you want to play one of the big boys at Bennington's? You want to leave off this penny-ante hustling and try and clean up in one big lick?"

"Who else is gonna let me win ten thousand in one night?"

"Look, Eddie." Charlie turned to him, his face still impassive. "You're not gonna charm those Chicago boys into a thing. Like in Hot Springs, only worse. You're gonna be playing people who know what's happening on a pool table."

"In Hot Springs I made a bad bet. I learned something. I won't make any bad bets in Chicago."

"I heard people say that when you walk in Bennington's you're making a bad bet."

Eddie, abruptly, laughed. "Charlie," he said, "if you wasn't my best friend, I'd make you get out and walk."

They drove silently for a while. It was getting late in the afternoon, the air was beginning to cool off now and there was more shade. They were passing clumps of buildings, getting into country that was more thickly settled. Traffic in the other direction was becoming thicker too, the beginnings of the weekend exodus from the city. Billboards hustling beer and gasoline became frequent.

Finally Charlie spoke. Eddie had been waiting for it, wondering exactly what it was that he had on his mind. "Eddie," he said, "you don't have to go to Bennington's at all. Why risk what we got? You can scuffle around in the little rooms and pick up at least a thousand, no chance of losing. Then we drive back home by a different way and you fill out your fifteen grand the same way you picked up what we already got."

Eddie let it all sink in. Then he said, almost pleadingly, "Charlie, you're trying to undermine my confidence. You know I got to play at Bennington's. You know I been a scuffler all my life, a small man out West. You know when I beat Johnny Varges—that's *Johnny Varges,* Charlie, the man who *invented* one-pocket pool—he said I was the best he ever seen. And back home there were people who said I was the best in the country. The best in the country, Charlie."

"That's right," Charlie said, "and you let a nowhere bank hustler named Woody Fleming hit you for eight hundred dollars in Hot Springs."

"Charlie," Eddie said, "I *gave* him two balls out of eight. For Christ's sake, that's the first money I dropped since we left Oakland, California."

"Okay. I take it back. I wanted to remind you that, sometimes, people lose."

Eddie's voice was still pained. "Look, Charlie. Did you ever see a better pool player than me? Did you ever see, in twenty years running a poolroom, anybody ever who I couldn't beat, heads up, any day of the week, any game of pool he could name?"

"Okay. Okay." A trace of irritation insinuated itself into Charlie's voice. "Nobody can beat you."

They passed through a suburb, then another. Eddie kept

smoking continually, and he was beginning to feel intensely a thing that he had felt many times before, but never before quite so strongly: a kind of electric self-awareness, a fine, alert tension. And a sense of anxiety, too, and of expectation. He felt good. Nervous; his stomach tight; but good.

5

EDDIE SAT ON THE EDGE OF THE BED, dressed only in his expensive shorts, in which he had slept. His bed was beside the window of the room and he was looking out, into the afternoon sunshine and into a tangle of the flat sides of buildings. Behind him, Charlie was still sleeping, his face, even in sleep, comic and impassive.

Eddie lit a cigarette, in a more leisurely way than he usually lit them. He felt good. He had just awakened from a long, mildly alcoholic sleep; but his mind had been instantly clear, the meaning of the time and the place understood.

He looked around the hotel room. It was very clean, modern-looking, with blond furniture and pastel walls; and this pleased him. He began whistling through his teeth.

Then he went to the bathroom and took a hot shower, washed his hair, scrubbed his fingernails with a pink nylon brush that he carried in his shaving kit, shaved, sat on the edge of the bathtub and began shining his shoes.

Charlie padded into the bathroom, wearing pajamas, and seated himself on the commode. He blinked at Eddie a minute, and at length spoke. "For Chrissake who—who else in God's green world in the morning would sit on the bathtub, naked as sin and with his ribs showing, and polish his goddamn shoes?" Then he fell into a classic pose of contemplation, elbows on knees.

Eddie finished with the shoebrush. "Me. And it's afternoon. Two o'clock in the afternoon."

"Okay," Charlie said. "Okay, so it's afternoon and that makes it just fine to parade your anatomy and shine your shoes in the bathtub. Okay. Now get out. I want privacy."

Eddie picked up his shoes and walked out of the bathroom, intentionally not closing the door. Charlie said nothing, but managed to reach a fat foot out far enough from his throne to slam it shut.

Eddie put on a pair of clean shorts and sat back down on the bed. Then he called out, as casually and as jokingly as he could, "How much money am I gonna win today, Charlie?"

He hadn't expected an answer; but he waited for one. Then he said, louder, "Who's gonna beat me?"

This, too, got no answer. Not from the sitting Buddha. But he felt high, and he felt like talking, like needling Charlie. He knew he had talked it up much too much already; but he wanted to talk it up more, wanted Charlie to try to puncture his ego for him more, wanted to laugh at Charlie and to know, too, that everything that Charlie said about him was right.

"What do you think Bennington's boys are gonna do when

they see me?" He leaned back on the bed, grinning; but his grin was a little tense, strained.

Charlie opened the door, waddled in, and began searching through his suitcase. "I already told you what I think about Bennington's," he said.

"Sure. But what about Bennington's boys? George the Fairy? Fats? They couldn't of helped but hear of me. And somebody'll finger me if they don't know me when they see me. What's gonna happen?"

Charlie found his toothbrush in the bag and held it up, pulling the lint out of it. "Look," he said, "you know as much about that as I do. And you know more about hustling than I ever did."

"Sure, but . . ."

"Look, Eddie." Charlie stood up, holding the toothbrush. The combination of pajamas and toothbrush made him look ridiculous, like a fat child in an advertisement. "This is all your idea. I said I'd take you around on the road, because I been on the road myself. And I taught you all I knew about scuffling in the little rooms—and it didn't take me a week to do that. But I didn't say I could steer you in this town. I heard of Minnesota Fats for fifteen years. I heard him called the best straight pool player in the country for fifteen years, but I wouldn't know him on the street if I saw him. And I don't know how good he is—all I know is his reputation. For Chrissake," he began heading back for the bathroom, "I don't know yet how good *you* are."

Eddie watched him walk toward the bathroom and open the door. Then he said, softly, "Well, I don't either, Charlie."

6

THEY HAD TO TAKE AN ELEVATOR to the eighth floor, an elevator that jerked and had brass doors and held five people. It did not seem at all right to go to a poolroom on an elevator; and he had never figured Bennington's that way. Nobody had ever told him about the elevator. When they stepped off it there was a very high, wide doorway facing them. Over this was written, in small, feeble neon letters, BENNINGTON'S BILLIARD HALL. He looked at Charlie and then they walked in.

Eddie had with him a small, cylindrical leather case. This was as big around as his forearm and about two and a half feet long. In it was an extremely well-made, inlaid, ivory-pointed, French-leather-tipped, delicately balanced pool cue. This was actually in two parts; they could be joined for use by screwing together a two-piece, machined brass joint, fastened to the maple end of each section.

The place was big, bigger, even than he had imagined. It was familiar, because the smell and the feel of a poolroom are the same everywhere; but it was also very much different. Victorian, with heavy, leather-cushioned chairs, big elaborate brass chandeliers, three high windows with heavy curtains, a sense of spaciousness, of elegance.

It was practically empty. No one plays pool late in the afternoon; few people come in at that time except to drink at the bar, make bets on the races or play the pinball machines; and Bennington's had facilities for none of these. This, too, was unique; its business was pool, nothing else.

There was a man practicing on the front table, a big man, smoking a cigar. On another table further back two tall children in blue jeans and jackets were playing nine ball. One of these had long sideburns. In the middle of the room a very big man with heavy, black-rimmed glasses—like an advertising executive—was sitting in an oak swivel chair by the cash register, reading a newspaper. He looked at them a moment after they came in and when he saw the leather case in Eddie's hand he stared for a moment at Eddie's face before going back to the paper. Beyond him, in the back of the room, a stooped black man in formless clothes was pushing a broom, limping.

They picked a table toward the back, several tables down from the nine-ball players, and began to practice. Eddie took a house cue stick from the rack, setting the leather case, unopened, against the wall.

They shot around, loosely, for about forty-five minutes. He was trying to get the feel of the table, to get used to the big four-and-a-half-by-nine-feet size—since the war practically all pool tables were four by eight—and to learn the bounce of the rails. They were a little soft and the nap on the cloth was smooth, making the balls take long angles and making stiffening English difficult. But the table was a good one, level, even, with clean pocket drops, and he liked the sense of it.

The big man with the cigar ambled down, took a chair, and watched them. Then after they had finished the game he took the cigar out of his mouth, looked at Eddie, very hard, looked at the leather case leaning against the wall, looked back at Eddie and said, thoughtfully, "You looking for action?"

Eddie smiled at him. "Maybe. You want to play?"

The big man scowled. "No. Hell, no." Then he said, "You Eddie Felson?"

Eddie grinned, "Who's he?" He took a cigarette out of his shirt pocket.

The man put the cigar back in his mouth. "What's your game? What do you shoot?"

Eddie lit the cigarette. "You name it, mister. We'll play."

The big man jerked the cigar from his mouth. "Look, friend," he said, "I'm not trying to hustle. I don't never hustle people who carry leather satchels in poolrooms." His voice was loud, commanding, and yet it sounded tired, as if he were greatly discouraged. "I ask you a civil question and you play it cute. I come up and watch and I think maybe I can help you out, and you want to be cute."

"Okay," Eddie grinned, "no hard feelings. I shoot straight pool. You know any straight pool players around this poolroom?"

"What kind of straight pool game do you like?"

Eddie looked at him a minute, noticing the way the man's eyes blinked. Then he said, "I like the expensive kind."

The man chewed on his cigar a minute. Then he leaned forward in his chair and said, "You come up here to play straight pool with Minnesota Fats?"

Eddie liked this man. He seemed very strange, as if he were going to explode. "Yes," he said.

The man stared at him, chewing the cigar. Then he said, "Don't. Go home."

"Why?"

"I'll tell you why, and you better believe it. Fats don't need your money. And there's no way you can beat him. He's the best in the country." He leaned back in the chair, blowing out smoke.

Eddie kept grinning. "I'll think about that," he said. "Where is he?"

The big man came alive, violently. "For God's sake," he said, loudly, despairingly, "You talk like a real high-class pool hustler. Who do you think you are—Humphrey Bogart? Maybe you carry a rod and wear raincoats and really hold a mean pool stick back in California or Idaho or wherever it is. I bet you already beat every nine-ball shooting farmer from here to the West Coast. Okay. I told you what I wanted about Minnesota Fats. You just go ahead and play him, friend."

Eddie laughed. Not scornfully, but with amusement—amusement at the other man and at himself. "All right," he said, laughing. "Just tell me where I find him."

The big man pulled himself up from the chair with considerable effort. "Just stay where you are," he said. "He comes in, every night, about eight o'clock." He jammed the cigar in his mouth and walked back to the front table.

"Thanks," Eddie called at him. The man didn't reply. He began practicing again, a long rail shot on the three ball.

Eddie and Charlie returned to their game. The talk with the big man could have rattled him but, somehow, it had the effect of making him feel better about the evening. He began concentrating on the game, getting his stroke down to a finer point, running little groups of balls and then missing intentionally—more from long habit than from fear of being identified. They kept shooting, and after a while the other tables began to fill up with men and smoke and the clicking of pool balls and he began to glance toward the massive front door, watching.

And then, after he had finished running a group of balls, he looked up and saw, leaning against the next table, an extremely fat man with black curly hair, watching him shoot—a man with small black eyes.

He picked up the chalk and began stroking his cue tip with it, slowly, looking at the man. It couldn't have been anyone else, not with all of that weight, not with the look of authority, not with those sharp little eyes.

He was wearing a silk sport shirt, chartreuse, open at the neck and loose on his wide, soft-looking belly. His face was like dough, like the face of the full moon on a free calendar, puffed up like an Eskimo's, little ears close to his head, the hair shiny, curly, and carefully trimmed, the complexion clear, pinkish. His hands were clasped over the great belly, above a small, jeweled belt buckle, and there were brightly jeweled rings on four of his fingers. The nails were manicured and polished.

About every ten seconds there was a sudden, convulsive motion of his head, forcing his chins down toward his left collar bone. This was a very sudden movement, and it brought an automatic grimace to that side of his mouth which seemed affected by the tic. Other than this there was no expression on his face.

The man stared back at him. Then he said, "You shoot pretty good straights." His voice had no tone whatever. It was very deep.

Eddie, somehow, did not feel like grinning. "Thanks," he said.

He turned back to the table and finished up the rack of balls. Then when the cashier, the man with the black-rimmed glasses, was racking them up, Eddie turned back to the fat man and said, smiling this time, "You play straight pool, mister?"

The man's chin jerked, abruptly, "Every once in a while," he said. "You know how it is." His voice sounded as though he were talking from the bottom of a well.

Eddie continued chalking his cue. "You're Minnesota Fats, aren't you, mister?"

The man said nothing, but his eyes seemed to flicker, as if he were amused, or trying to be amusing.

Eddie kept smiling, but he felt his fingertips quivering and put one hand in his pocket, holding the cue stick with the other. "They say Minnesota Fats is the best in the country, out where I come from," he said.

"Is that a fact?" The man's face jerked again.

"That's right," Eddie said. "Out where I come from they say Minnesota Fats shoots the eyes right off them balls."

The other man was quiet for a minute. Then he said, "You come from California, don't you?"

"That's right."

"Name of Felson, Eddie Felson?" He pronounced the words carefully, distinctly, with neither warmth nor malice in them.

"That's right too."

There seemed nothing more to say. Eddie went back to his game with Charlie. Knowing Fats was watching him, adding him up, calculating the risks of playing him, he felt nervous; but his hands were steady with the cue and the nervousness was only enough to make him feel alert, springy, to sharpen his sense of the game he was playing, his feel for the balls and for the roll of the balls and the swing of the cue. He laid it on carefully, disregarding his normal practice of making himself look weak, shooting well-controlled, neat shots, until the fifteen colored balls were gone from the table.

Then he turned around and looked at Fats. Fats seemed not to see him. His chin jerked, and then he turned to a small man who had been standing next to him, watching, and said, "He shoots straight. You think maybe he's a hustler?" Then he turned back to Eddie, his face blank but the little eyes sharp, watching. "You a gambler, Eddie?" he said. "You like to gamble money on pool games?"

Eddie looked him full in the face and, abruptly, grinned. "Fats," he said, grinning, feeling good, all the way, "let's you and me play a game of straight pool."

Fats looked at him a moment. Then he said, "Fifty dollars?"

Eddie laughed, looked at Charlie and then back again, "Hell, Fats," he said, "you shoot big-time pool. Everybody says you shoot big-time pool. Let's don't be chicken about this." He looked at the men standing by Fats. Both of them were bugged, astonished. *Probably,* he thought, *nobody's ever talked to their big tin god like this before.* He grinned. "Let's make it a hundred, Fats."

Fats stared at him, his expression unchanging. Then, suddenly, with a great moving of flesh, he smiled. "They call you Fast Eddie, don't they?" he said.

"That's right." Eddie was still grinning.

"Well, Fast Eddie. You talk my kind of talk. You flip a coin so we see who breaks."

Eddie took his leather case from where it was leaning against the wall.

Someone flipped a half dollar. Eddie lost the toss and had to break the balls. He took the standard shot—two balls out from the rack and back again, three rails on the cue ball to the end cushion—and he froze the cue ball on the rail with only a bare edge of a corner ball sticking from behind the rack, to shoot at. Then Fats walked very slowly, ponderously, up to the front of the poolroom, where there was a green metal locker. He opened this and took out a cue stick, one joined at the middle with a brass joint, like Eddie's. He picked a cube of chalk up from the front table and chalked his cue as he walked back. He did not even appear to look at the position of the balls on the table, but merely said, "Five ball. Corner pocket," and took his position behind the cue ball to shoot.

Eddie watched him closely. He stepped up to the table with short, quick little steps, stepping up to it sideways, bringing his cue up into position as he did so, so that he was holding his cue, standing sideways to the table, out across his great stomach, the left-hand bridge already formed, the right hand holding the butt delicately, much as a violinist holds his bow—gracefully but surely. And then, as if it were an integral, continuous part of his approach to the table, his bridge hand settled down on the green and almost immediately there was a smooth, level motion of the cue stick, effortless, and the cue ball sped down the table and clipped the corner of the five ball and the five ball sped across the table and into the corner pocket. The cue ball darted into the rack, spreading the balls wide.

And then Fats began moving around the table, making balls, all of his former ponderousness gone now, his motions like a ballet, the steps light, sure, and rehearsed; the bridge hand inevitably falling into the right place; the hand on the butt of the cue with its fat, jeweled fingers gently pushing the thin shaft into the cue ball. He never stopped to look at the layout of the balls, never appeared to think or to prepare himself for shooting. About every five shots he stopped long enough to stroke the tip of his cue gently with chalk; but he did not even look at the table as he did this; he merely watched what he was doing at the moment.

He made fourteen out of the fifteen balls on the table very quickly, leaving the remaining ball in excellent position for the break.

Eddie racked the balls. Fats made the break shot, shooting effortlessly but powering the cue ball into the rack so that it scattered balls all over the table. He began punching them in. He was good. He was fantastically good. He ran eighty balls before he got tied up and played Eddie safe. Eddie had seen and made bigger runs, much bigger; but he had never seen anyone shoot with the ease, the unruffled certainty, that this delicate, gross man had.

Eddie looked at Charlie, sitting now in one of the big, high chairs. Charlie's face showed nothing, but he shrugged his shoulders. Then Eddie looked the shot over carefully. It was a good safe, but he was able to return it, freezing the cue ball to the end rail, leaving nothing to be shot at. They played it back and forth, safe, leaving no openings for the other man, until Eddie made a small slip and let Fats get loose. Fats edged up to the table and started shooting. Eddie sat down. He looked around; a crowd of ten or fifteen people had already formed around the table. A neat man with pink cheeks and glasses was moving around in the crowd, making bets. Eddie wondered what on. He looked at the clock on the wall over the door. It was eight-thirty. He took a deep breath, and then let it out slowly.

He had known he would start out losing. That was natural; he was playing a great player and on his own table, in his own poolroom, and he figured to lose for a few hours. But not that badly. Fats beat him two games by one hundred and twenty-five to nothing and in the third game Eddie finally got one open shot and scored fifty on it. It was not pleasant to lose, and yet, somehow, he was not deeply dismayed, did not feel lost in the brilliance of the other man's game, did not feel nervous or confused. He spent most of each game sitting down and each time Fats won a game Eddie grinned and gave him a hundred dollars. Fats had nothing to say.

At eleven o'clock, after he had lost the sixth game, Charlie came over, looked at him, and said, "Quit."

He looked at Charlie, who seemed to be perspiring, and said, "I'll take him. Just wait."

"Don't be too sure." Charlie went back to his chair, on the other side of the table.

Then Eddie started winning. He felt it start in the middle of a game, began to feel the sense he sometimes had of being a part of the table and of the balls and of the cue stick. The stroke of his arm seemed to travel on oiled bearings; and each muscle of his body was alert, sensitive to the game and the movement of the balls, sharply aware of how every ball would roll, of how, exactly, every shot must be made. Fats beat him that game, but he had felt it coming and he won the next.

And the game after that, and the next, and then another. Then someone turned off all the lights except those over the table that they were playing on and the background of Bennington's vanished, leaving only the faces of the crowd around the table, the green of the cloth of the table, and the now sharply etched, clean, black-shadowed balls, brilliant against the green. The balls had sharp, jeweled edges; the cue ball itself was a milk-white jewel and it was a magnificent thing to watch the balls roll and to know beforehand where they were going to roll. Nothing could be so clear or so simple or so excellent to do. And there was no limit to the shots that could be made.

Fats' game did not change. It was brilliant, fantastically good, but Eddie was beating him now, playing an incredible game: a gorgeous, spellbinding game, a game that he felt he had known all of his life, that he would play when the right time came. There was no better time than this.

And then, after a game had ended, there was noise up front and Eddie turned and saw that the clock said midnight and that someone was locking the great oak door, and he looked at Fats and Fats said, "Don't worry, Fast Eddie. We're not going anyplace."

Then he pulled a ten-dollar bill out of his pocket, handed it to a thin nervous man in a black suit, who was watching the game, and said, "Preacher, I want White Horse whiskey. And ice. And a glass. And you get yourself a fix with the change; but you do that after you come back with my whiskey."

Eddie grinned, liking the feel of this, the getting ready for action. He fished out a ten himself. "J. T. S. Brown bourbon," he said to the thin man. Then he leaned his cue stick against the table, unbuttoned his cuffs, and began rolling up his shirt sleeves. Then he stretched out his arms, flexing the muscles, enjoying the good sense of their steadiness, their control, and he said, "Okay, Fats. Your break."

Eddie beat him. The pleasure was exquisite; and when the man brought the whiskey and he mixed himself a highball with water from the cooler and drank it, his whole body and brain seemed to be suffused with pleasure, with alertness and life. He looked at Fats. There was a dark line of sweat and dirt around the back of his collar. His manicured nails were dirty. His face still showed no expression. He, too, was holding a glass of whiskey and sipping it quietly.

Suddenly Eddie grinned at him. "Let's play for a thousand a game, Fats," he said.

There was a murmur in the crowd.

Fats took a sip of whiskey, rolled it around carefully in his mouth, swallowed. His sharp, black eyes were fixed on Eddie, dispassionately, searching. He seemed to see something there that reassured him. Then he glanced, for a moment, at the neat man with glasses, the man who had been taking bets. The man nodded, pursing his lips. "Okay," he said.

Eddie knew it, could feel it, that no one had ever played straight pool like this before. Fats' game, itself, was astonishing, a consistently beautiful, precise game, a deft, quick shooting game with almost no mistakes. And he won games; no power on earth could have stopped him from winning some of them, for pool is a game that gives the man sitting down no earthly way of affecting the shooting of the man he is trying to beat. But Eddie beat him, steadily, making shots that no one had ever made before, knifing balls in, playing hairline position, running rack after rack of balls without his cue ball's touching a cushion, firing ball after ball into the center, the heart of every pocket. His stroking arm was like a conscious thing, and the cue stick was a living extension of it. There were nerves in the wood of it, and he could feel the tapping of the leather tip with the nerves, could feel the balls roll; and the exquisite sound that they made as they hit the bottoms of the pockets was a sound both there, on the table, and in the very center of his own soul.

They played for a long, long time and then he noticed that the shadows of the balls on the green had become softer, had lost their edges. He looked up and saw pale light coming through the window draperies and then looked at the clock. It was seven-thirty. He looked around him, dazed. The crowd had thinned out, but some of the same men were there. Everybody seemed to need a shave. He felt his own face. Sandpaper. He looked down at himself. His shirt was filthy, covered with chalk marks, the tail out, and the front wrinkled as if he had slept in it. He looked at Fats, who looked, if anything, worse.

Charlie came over. He looked like hell too. He blinked at Eddie. "Breakfast?"

Eddie sat down, in one of the now-empty chairs by the table. "Yeah," he said. "Sure." He fished in his pocket, pulled out a five.

"Thanks," Charlie said. "I don't need it. I been keeping the money, remember?"

Eddie grinned, weakly. "That's right. How much is it now?"

Charlie stared at him. "You don't know?"

"I forgot." He fished a crumpled cigarette from his pocket, lit it. His hands, he noticed, were trembling faintly; but he saw this as if he were looking at someone else. "What is it?" He leaned back, smoking the cigarette, looking at the balls sitting, quiet now, on the table. The cigarette had no taste to it.

"You won eleven thousand four hundred," Charlie said. "Cash. It's in my pocket."

Eddie looked back at him. "Well!" he said. And then, "Go get breakfast. I want a egg sandwich and coffee."

"Now wait a minute," Charlie said. "You're going with me. We eat breakfast at the hotel. The pool game is over."

Eddie looked at him a minute, grinning, wondering, too, why it was that Charlie couldn't see it, never had seen it. Then he leaned forward, looked at him, and said, "No it isn't, Charlie."

"Eddie . . ."

"This pool game ends when Minnesota Fats says it ends."

"You came after ten thousand. You got ten thousand."

Eddie leaned forward again. He wasn't grinning now. He wanted Charlie to see it, to get with it, to feel some of what he was feeling, some of the commitment he was making. "Charlie," he said, "I came here after Minnesota Fats. And I'm gonna get him. I'm gonna stay with him all the way."

Fats was sitting down, too, resting. He stood up. His chin jerked, down into the soft flesh of his neck. "Fast Eddie," he said tonelessly, "let's play pool."

"Break the balls," Eddie said.

In the middle of the game the food came and Eddie ate his sandwich in bites between shots, setting it on the rail of the table while he was shooting, and washing it down with the coffee, which tasted very bitter. Fats had sent someone out and he was eating from a platter of a great many small sandwiches and link sausages. Instead of coffee he had three bottles of Dutch beer on another platter and these he drank from a pilsner glass, which he held in a fat hand, delicately. He wiped his lips gently with a napkin between bites of the sandwiches and, apparently, paid no attention whatever to the balls that Eddie was methodically pocketing in the thousand-dollar game that he, sitting in the chair and eating his gourmet's breakfast, was playing in.

Eddie won the game; but Fats won the next one, by a narrow margin. And at nine o'clock the poolroom doors were opened again and an ancient colored man limped in and began sweeping the floor and opened the windows, pulling back the draperies. Outside the sky was, absurdly, blue. The sun shone in.

Fats turned his head toward the janitor and said, his voice loud and flat, across the room, "Cut off that goddamn sunshine."

The black man shuffled back to the windows and drew the curtains. Then he went back to his broom.

They played, and Eddie kept winning. In his shoulders, now, and in his back and at the backs of his legs there was a kind of dull pain; but the pain seemed as if it were someone else's and he hardly felt it, hardly knew it was there. He merely kept shooting and the balls kept falling and the grotesque, fat man whom he was playing—the man who was the Best Straight Pool Player in the Country—kept giving large amounts of money to Charlie. Once, he noticed that, while he was shooting and the other man was sitting, Fats was talking with the man with the pink cheeks and with Gordon, the manager. The pink-cheeked man had his billfold in his hand. After that game, Fats paid Charlie with a thousand-dollar bill. The sight of the bill that he had just earned made him feel nothing. He only wished that the rack man would hurry and rack the balls.

The aching and the dullness increased gradually; but these did not affect the way his body played pool. There was a strange, exhilarating feeling that he was really somewhere else in the room, above the table—floating, possibly, with the heavy, bodiless mass of cigarette smoke that hung below the light—watching his own body, down below, driving small colored balls into holes by poking them with a long, polished stick of wood. And somewhere else in the room, perhaps everywhere in the room, was an incredibly fat man, silent, always in motion, unruffled, a man whose sharp little eyes saw not only the colored balls on the green rectangle, but saw also into all of the million corners in the room, whether or not they were illuminated by the cone of light that circumscribed the bright oblong of the pool table.

At nine o'clock in the evening Charlie told him that he had won eighteen thousand dollars.

Something happened, suddenly, in his stomach when Charlie told him this. A thin steel blade touched against a nerve in his stomach. He tried to look at Fats, but, for a moment, could not.

At ten-thirty, after winning one and then losing one, Minnesota Fats went back to the bathroom and Eddie found himself sitting down and then, in a moment, his head was in his hands and he was staring at the floor, at a little group of flat cigarette butts at his feet. And then Charlie was with him, or he heard his voice; but it seemed to be coming from a distance and when he tried to raise his head he could not. But Charlie was telling him to quit, he knew that without being able to pick out the word. And then the cigarette butts began to shift positions and to sway, in a gentle but confusing motion, and there was a humming in his ears like the humming of a cheap radio and, suddenly, he realized that he was passing out, and he shook his head, weakly at first and then violently, and when he stopped doing this he could see and hear better. But something in his mind was screaming. Something in him was quivering, frightened, cutting at his stomach from the inside, like a small knife.

Charlie was still talking but he broke him off, saying, "Give me a drink, Charlie." He did not look at Charlie, but kept his eyes on the cigarette butts, watching them closely.

"You don't need a drink."

Then he looked up at him, at the round, comic face dirty with beard and said, surprised at the softness of his own voice, "Shut up, Charlie. Give me a drink."

Charlie handed him the bottle.

He turned it up and let the whiskey spill down his throat. It gagged him but he did not feel it burn, hardly felt it in his stomach except as a mild warmness, softening the edges of the knife. Then he looked around him and found that his vision was all right, that he could see clearly the things directly in front of him, although there was a mistiness around the edges.

Fats was standing by the table, cleaning his fingernails. His hands were clean again; he had washed them; and his hair although still greasy, dirty looking, was combed. He seemed no more tired—except for the soiled shirt and a slight squinting of the eyes—than he had when Eddie had first seen him. Eddie looked away, looking back at the pool table. The balls were racked into their neat triangle. The cue ball sat at the head of the table, near the side rail, in position for the break.

Fats was at the side of his vision, in the misty part, and he appeared to be smiling placidly. "Let's play pool, Fast Eddie," he said.

Suddenly, Eddie turned to him and stared. Fats' chin jerked, toward his shoulder, his mouth twisting with the movement. Eddie watched this and it seemed, now, to have some kind of meaning; but he did not know what the meaning was.

And then he leaned back in his chair and said, the words coming almost without volition, "I'll beat you, Fats."

Fats just looked at him.

Eddie was not sure whether or not he was grinning at the fat man, at the huge, ridiculous, effeminate, jeweled ballet dancer of a pool hustler, but he felt as if something were going to make him laugh aloud at any minute. "I'll beat you, Fats," he said. "I beat you all day and I'll beat you all night."

"Let's play pool, Fast Eddie."

And then it came, the laughing. Only it was like someone else laughing, not himself, so that he heard himself as if it were from across the room. And then there were tears in his eyes, misting over his vision, fuzzing together the poolroom, the crowd of people around him, and the fat man, into a meaningless blur of colors, shaded with a dark, dominating green that seemed, now, to be actually being diffused from the surface of the table. And then the laughing stopped and he blinked at Fats.

He said it very slowly, tasting the words thickly as they came on. "I'm the best you ever seen, Fats." That was it. It was very simple. "I'm the best there is." He had known it, of course, all along, for years. But now it was so clear, so simple, that no one—not even Charlie—could mistake it. "I'm the best. Even if you beat me, I'm the best." The mistiness was clearing from his eyes again and he could see Fats standing sideways at the table, laying his hand down toward the green, not even aiming. *Even if you beat me . . .*

Somewhere in Eddie, deep in him, a weight was being lifted away. And, deeper still, there was a tiny, distant voice, a thin, anguished cry that said to him, sighing, *You don't have to win.* For hours there had been the weight, pressing on him, trying to break him, and now these words, this fine and deep and true revelation, had come and were taking the weight from him. The weight of responsibility. And the small steel knife of fear.

He looked back at the great fat man. "I'm the best," he said, "no matter who wins."

"We'll see," Fats said, and he broke the balls.

When Eddie looked at the clock again it was a little past midnight. He lost two in a row. Then he won one, lost one, won another—all of them close scores. The pain in his right upper arm seemed to glow outward from the bone and his shoulder was a lump of heat with swollen blood vessels around it and the cue stick seemed to mush into the cue ball when he hit it. And the balls no longer clicked when they hit one another but seemed to hit as if they were made of balsa wood. But he still could not miss the balls; it was still ridiculous that anyone could miss them; and his eyes saw the balls in sharp, brilliant detail although there seemed to be no longer a range of sensitivity to his vision. He felt he could see in the dark or could look at, stare into, the sun—the brightest sun at full noon—and stare it out of the sky.

He did not miss; but when he played safe, now, the cue ball did not always freeze against the rail or against a cluster of balls as he wanted it to. Once, at a critical time in a game, when he had to play safe, the cue ball rolled an inch too far and left Fats an open shot and Fats ran sixty-odd balls and out. And later, during what should have been a big run, he miscalculated a simple, one-rail position roll and had to play for defense. Fats won that game too. When he did, Eddie said, "You fat son of a bitch, you make mistakes expensive."

But he kept on making them. He would still make large numbers of balls but something would go wrong and he would throw the advantage away. And Fats didn't make mistakes. Not ever. And then Charlie came over after a game, and said, "Eddie, you still got the ten thousand. But that's all. Let's quit and go home. Let's go to bed."

Eddie did not look at him. "No," he said.

"Look, Eddie," he said, his voice soft, tired, "what is it you want to do? You beat him. You beat him bad. You want to kill yourself?"

Eddie looked up at him. "What's the matter, Charlie?" he said, trying to grin at him. "You chicken?"

Charlie looked back at him for a minute before he spoke. "Yeah," he said, "maybe that's it. I'm chicken."

"Okay. Then go home. Give me the money."

"Go to hell."

Eddie held his hand out. "Give me the money, Charlie. It's mine."

Charlie just looked at him. Then he reached in his pocket and pulled out a tremendous roll of money, wrinkled bills rolled up and wrapped with a heavy rubber band.

"Here," he said. "Be a goddamn fool."

Eddie stuffed the roll in his pocket. When he stood up to play he looked down at himself. It seemed grossly funny; one pocket bulging with a whiskey bottle, the other with paper money.

It took a slight effort to pick up his cue and start playing again; but after he started the playing did not seem to stop. He did not even seem to be aware of the times when he was sitting down and Fats was shooting, seemed always to be at the table himself, stroking with his bruised, screaming arm, watching the bright little balls roll and spin and twist their ways about the table. But, although he was hardly aware that Fats was shooting, he knew that he was losing, that Fats was winning more games than he was. And when the janitor came in to open up the poolroom and sweep the floor and they had to stop playing for a few minutes while he swept the cigarette butts from around the table, Eddie sat down to count his money. He could not count it, could not keep track of what he had counted; but he could see that the roll was much smaller than it had been when Charlie gave it to him. He looked at

Fats and said, "You fat bastard. You fat lucky bastard," but Fats said nothing.

And then, after a game, Eddie counted off a thousand dollars to Fats, holding the money on the table, under the light, and when he had counted off the thousand he saw that there were only a few bills left. This did not seem right, and he had to look for a moment before he realized what it meant. Then he counted them. There was a hundred-dollar bill, two fifties, a half-dozen twenties and some tens and ones.

Something happened in his stomach. A fist had clamped on something in his stomach and was twisting it.

"All right," he said. "All right, Fats. We're not through yet. We'll play for two hundred. Two hundred dollars a game." He looked at Fats, blinking now, trying to bring his eyes to focus on the huge man across the table from him. "Two hundred dollars. That's a hustler's game of pool."

Fats was unscrewing his cue, unfastening the brass joint in its center. He looked at Eddie. "The game's over," he said.

Eddie leaned over the table, letting his hand fall on the cue ball. "You can't quit me," he said.

Fats did not even look at him. "Watch," he said.

Eddie looked around. The crowd was beginning to leave the table, men were shuffling away, breaking up into little groups, talking. Charlie was walking toward him, his hands in his pockets. The distance between them seemed very great, as though he were looking down a long hallway.

Abruptly, Eddie pushed himself away from the table, clutching the cue ball in his hand. He felt himself staggering. "Wait!" he said. Somehow, he could not see, and the sounds were all melting into one another. “Wait!” He could barely hear his own voice. Somehow, he swung his arm, his burning, swollen, throbbing right arm, and he heard the cue ball crash against the floor and then he was on the floor himself and could see nothing but a lurching motion around him, unclear patterns of light swinging around his head, and he was vomiting, on the floor and on the front of his shirt. . . .

7

HE AWOKE AT FOUR O'CLOCK in the morning. He awoke with perspiration sticky on his face and with the taste of acid and vomit in his mouth, awoke from a long dream of a bright light and a thousand spinning colored balls, awoke but kept his mind, for minutes, at the edge of the remembrance of what had happened before he had come back to the hotel and had fallen into bed.

And then he tried to sit up—still not letting himself remember—and the surprise of the pain in his arms and his back, together with the unreality of awaking at four o'clock in the morning in a strange city, perspiring, wearing shoes in bed, the surprise of these things jarred the memory loose and it took hold of him, burning. He fell back and stared into the darkness, every scene of his stupidity and arrogance before him, in sharp detail, seen as clearly, as circumscribed by his own free will and choice to be a fool, as had the circle of light above the table at Bennington's encompassed the ground where he had chosen—deliberately and with no one else to blame—to play the fool and play him well.

But this kind of vision does not last long. Maybe the light is too bright, too clear, and hurts the eyes. Eddie Felson pushed himself up painfully in bed and sat on the edge of it, his mind now a blank, waiting for the thick, phlegmatic ache at the base of his brain and the ache that burned the length of his right arm to go away. But they did not and he had to force himself erect. He did not feel that he could stand the light to be on and he shuffled and bumped his way across the room and into the bathroom. His feet felt as if they had been swathed with thick bandages and stuffed into his shoes. He managed to turn the water faucet on and stick his head under it. The water was hot, and he fumbled with the faucets, adjusting it. Then he withdrew his head, sopping, and groped for a towel. He turned the light on and, after a minute of squinting, looked in the mirror.

It was somebody else's face. The eyes grotesquely puffed, the hair dripping, clinging to the forehead, the neck dirty, smeared chalk on the forehead, the lips cracked, blistered. Somehow he managed a faint grin. "You son of a bitch," he said, "you look like hell."

Then he took a hand towel, a white one, from the rack over the lavatory, wadded it up in the bowl, sopped it with steaming water, rubbed it with a cake of soap, and began scrubbing his face. Then he washed the back of his neck—holding his head over the bowl—and the sweaty area under his chin. This soaked his collar, making it stick to his neck, and he stopped long enough to take his shirt and undershirt off. He washed his chest and arms then, holding the hot cloth around his right shoulder until the aching was dulled by it. After this he tore a hotel washcloth from its cellophane package and began washing his face more carefully, in greater detail, rubbing hard at the places where the chalk marks were, using more soap, getting every vestige of the finely powdered green from his skin.

When he was satisfied with this, his face glowing and his upper body chilled, dripping, but purified, he filled the bowl and stuck his head in it, soaking his hair in the warm, soapy liquid. He withdrew his head, squinted burning eyes, sneezed the water from his nose, and began scrubbing at the hair, scraping through it violently with his fingernails—knowing that he was cleaning them, too, of the filth and talcum powder and green chalk and shame that were under them.

Standing back from the loudly draining bowl, he grabbed a dry towel, sat on the edge of the tub, and began rubbing himself dry. The towel smelled faintly of Clorox, a strong, clean smell.

Then he shaved, slowly and carefully, and soaked his face afterward with a pungent, alcoholic lotion. He brushed his teeth with icy water, violence, and a stinging mint confection from a battered tube. He combed his hair, and when he had finished this looked in the mirror again, paused and said, "Anyway, now you're a good-looking son of a bitch."

Then he packed the lavatory tools into their case, went into the bedroom, opened his suitcase, put the toilet kit in, and withdrew a clean shirt and undershirt—both white—clean pants and socks. He put these on, wadded and stuffed the dirty things into the suitcase, and closed it.

He glanced at Charlie. Charlie was still completely flat.

Then he took out his billfold. In it were two hundred eighty-three dollars. He counted out one hundred fifty and then put the rest back in his pocket. He went to the bed where Charlie lay asleep, his face dirty, wearied, impassive. Next to the bed was a nightstand, with a cheap modern lamp on it. Eddie set the one hundred fifty in bills on the nightstand, making a neat little stack of the money. Then he fished in his pocket, withdrew the car keys, and set them on top of the bills. He looked at the sleeping man for a moment. "Okay, Charlie," he said softly, "I'll see you around." On the floor by his bed the leather case with the cue stick in it was lying. He picked it up by the handle, and then abruptly he turned back to Charlie and said, "Charlie, I'm sorry. . . ." Then he took his suitcase and left the room.

Outside, the sky was graying off, and somewhere a bird was singing, remote and feeble. From a window there was the sound of dance music, of talk. The air was pleasant and cool. A dog ran yipping up the middle of the street, its barking still echoing after it had turned a corner and was out of sight. He felt better, walking, but his mind was still thick, the pictures in it confused and unclear.

He tried not to think of anything except the simple fact that he was hungry. There was much else to think about, but this was not the time for thinking. After he had walked a few blocks he came to a bus station. In the waiting room were a scattering of very grubby, tired people—a woman with a red and ugly baby, some big-handed, dull-eyed men, a group of withdrawn old women, who seemed to be huddled against the brightness of the room itself. He did not like even seeing such people.

Along one wall there were public lockers—the gambler's

ubiquitous closet. He checked his bag and case in one of them. He looked at his watch. It said ten minutes until five.

The station lunchroom was less than half open. Most of it had been roped off and there were only five stools left at the counter and four booths along the wall. The stools were all filled; a pair of bus drivers on one side, three men in wrinkled business suits at the other. The lights were very bright; and the talking of the men seemed distant, yet highly articulate—strange, early-morning sounds, like the shrill conversations of birds that would soon begin outside.

In one of the booths only one person was sitting. This was a girl—a small, not very pretty girl—drinking coffee, alone. Eddie hesitated a moment and then sat down in the booth, facing her. She was staring at her coffee and did not look up at him. There was one waitress, a harried and skinny woman in a uniform, and he tried to catch her attention.

After a moment he turned back and looked at the girl. Beside her elbow was an ash tray, filled with cigarette butts. As he noticed this she pulled a silver case from the pocket of the tan coat she was wearing, withdrew a cigarette, and placed it between her lips. There was deftness in the motion—a kind of thing that Eddie always noticed when it appeared—and she lighted the cigarette with a smooth, easy movement. She did this without looking up from the coffee cup, into which she was staring.

This seemed to be an opening. He grinned and said, "Long wait for a bus?"

She lifted her eyes from the cup for a moment. He nodded toward the ash tray. "Yes," she said. Her voice was tired, the tone final. She returned to her coffee.

The light was very harsh and it was difficult to tell whether the hard set of her features was a consequence of the bright light and the shadows—or of other lights and other shadows. Her skin was very pale, and there were shadows beneath her eyes. Yet the eyes, although tired, were not actually dull; there was a hint of something alert about them.

Her hair was dark, cut short, practically straight. She could have been pretty, but she was not. Her lips were too pale, even with the faint lipstick she wore, and not full enough. There was a certain boyishness to her forehead; she had no discernible bosom; and the bone structure of her face, although fine and delicate, was too much in evidence. Or perhaps that was because of the light. Yet she did not look sickly; there was a suggestion of tired wakefulness, of self-sufficiency, about her.

He could not think of anything further to say and waited in silence for what seemed a long time, until the waitress came by, setting the universal glass of iceless water on the plastic table top before him. He ordered scrambled eggs, sausage, and coffee.

And then, on an impulse, he said, "Just a minute," and to the girl, "You want another cup of coffee?" He made his voice casual, as friendly as possible.

She raised her eyes again and he grinned at her with what he knew to be his most forthright and amiable grin. This was the grin which, together with his honest face, he relied upon when on the hustle.

She hesitated a moment, then shrugged gently. "Okay," she said, and then when the waitress was gone, "Thanks." She looked at his face quizzically. There was nothing at all about this look to imply either flirtation or avoidance of flirtation.

It was as if she were merely curious about what kind of man would be trying to pick her up in the bus station. Somehow this amused him.

He let the grin relax into a smile and said, "When does the bus leave?"

"What bus?"

"Yours."

"Oh." A private smile appeared on her face and then vanished. "Six o'clock."

He glanced at his watch. "You've got almost an hour," he said.

She nodded, and then finished the cup of coffee she had been drinking.

"How long you been waiting?" he said.

She turned her eyes up to him again. He liked the gesture; he had seen a girl in a movie do it that way once and he had liked it then. "Since four."

There seemed nothing more to say, and they became silent. He was a little confused by the girl; he did not know whether she had been friendly or not. He would let it ride, let her open the conversation again if she wanted to. Anyway, it was pointless if she was leaving town at six o'clock.

The waitress brought his breakfast and the coffee. He ate slowly and silently; his stomach seemed acutely conscious of the food. She stirred her coffee for a long while before she began sipping at it.

When he had finished the breakfast he began to feel more alive. There was still a sense of pain in him somewhere, the scars of the knife in his stomach; but now he felt tighter, more aware of what was happening. The ache in his right shoulder remained, however—a reminder of what the night's work had been.

He decided to try the girl again, for what she was worth. "Could I bum a cigarette?" he said.

"Sure." She handed him the case from her pocket. "You press the button at the end."

The case was heavy and plain; turning it over in his hand he saw the word "Sterling" stamped on its bottom. "This is nice," he said, opening it and taking out a cigarette. He handed it back to her.

When he lit the cigarette he noticed with surprise that his fingers were still trembling. His matches said BENNINGTON'S BILLIARD ROOM on them, in green letters.

The cigarette tasted like tar. He coughed from it, and then looked at it more closely. On it was printed GITANES. "What did you give me," he said, "marijuana?"

She smiled the faint smile again. "They're French."

"What for?"

She seemed to think a moment. "I don't know," she said, "to impress my friends, probably."

It was a peculiar answer, but sufficient. He continued smoking, gingerly. It did not taste so bad when he inhaled it gently.

When he stubbed out the cigarette and looked at his watch, it was a quarter of six. He looked at the girl; she was absorbed in studying her coffee again, stirring the remains of it idly with her spoon. This irritated him slightly and he thought, *What the hell.* He got up and said, "Have a good trip."

She looked up at him. "Thanks. I will." And as he was paying the check, "Thanks for the coffee."

Outside it was dirty, silver daylight and traffic sounds. The air was already becoming warm and moist. He felt neither sleepy nor hungry nor yet fully awake, and did not know what to do. He began walking, and a block from the bus station found a painted sign that said HOTEL FOR MEN. Inside, a fat Negress gave him a key to a seventh-floor cubicle. The room was surprisingly clean. He sat on the bed for more than an hour and thought and tried not to think about Minnesota Fats. This produced nothing. He did not feel like sleeping, got up finally, and went back out. There was more daylight, more traffic, more fast-walking people. He could think about Minnesota Fats—about the fat man, the pool game, and what they had all meant—later. Maybe in a few days, when he felt more like thinking it all out.

There had been a bar across the street from the bus station, closed before. It would probably be open now.

It was open, and there was a customer in it. In the back of the room, in a booth, the girl from the bus station. The lights were softer but it was the same scene, except that she was sipping a highball this time.

It seemed very strange, and for a moment it shook him. Then he walked back to her. She watched him coming, with the gesture of looking up at him. "Hello," he said, grinning. "Have a nice trip?" She looked much better, with the softer light on her face.

"Fair."

"Can I sit down?"

She did not smile; but her face did not seem so severe. "Why not," she said. "Already we know each other's secrets."

He eased into the seat, wondering what she had meant. Then he signaled the bartender for bourbon and water. He looked back to her, noticed that her drink was almost gone, and said, "Look, if I buy you a drink will you tell me why you didn't catch that bus?"

She looked at him a moment, and then for the first time smiled, wryly. "You can buy me a drink," she said, "but I'd tell you anyway."

He called to the bartender, "Another for the lady." Then he looked back at her. "Okay," he said, "why didn't you catch the bus?"

She leaned back against the plastic upholstery of the seat. The seat was high-backed, and against it she looked like a child on a large sofa. She reached a small hand forward and stirred her drink. "I wasn't waiting for a bus," she said.

The man brought them their drinks and Eddie sipped at his. It tasted delicious; the bourbon cold and clean, like a mild antiseptic.

"Then why go to the bus station?" he said.

"The same reason you went there, probably. At five in the morning you don't have much choice." It was either the liquor or the lights or the fact that she seemed to have accepted his presence: her face had become more relaxed, although there was still no act, no assumption of any particular relationship. Eddie wondered, briefly, what would happen if he got up and went to sit beside her, patted her on the butt or something. Probably nothing. She looked as if she could handle herself.

"Besides," she said, "I only live three blocks from here."

Was that an invitation of some sort? He looked at her closely. Not likely.

"And you like bus stations?"

"No. I hate bus stations." She made a small gesture with her hand. "Sometimes I wake up and I can't get back to sleep—not without a drink. And this bar doesn't open until six o'clock."

He liked the way she talked. Her voice was soft, yet the words were precise and well enunciated. There was something in the sound of her voice that, like the plain silver cigarette case, felt of natural class—a quality that Eddie liked very much.

"You always drink in the mornings?" he said.

"No. Only when I'm broke and have to wait for the bars to open so I can charge a drink. Otherwise I usually have a bottle at home. In which case I sleep very well."

This seemed ridiculous. She liked talking that way about herself. If she were really a lush she probably wouldn't talk about it.

He looked back at her and it struck him, suddenly, that she was pretty. Why not make a quick try, the fast hustle? "Look," he said, "I can buy us a bottle. . . ."

Her expression hardly changed; but her voice was like a wall. "No," she said.

"Say, a fifth of Scotch."

She leaned forward, "Look," she said, "we were doing fine here. Come off it." She took a draw from her cigarette. "Anyway, I'm not your type."

What she had said was instantly right and he grinned at her. "All right," he said. "You win. Sorry I brought it up."

"That's okay," she said, leaning back again. "A proposition is supposed to be flattering, even from a man who picks you up in a bus station. And I like Scotch—you made the right offer."

"Glad to hear it," he said. He finished off his drink and then said, "One more?"

"No," she said, "I'm sleepy now." She got up from her seat.

He stood up, too, and saw how short she was, smaller than she had looked to be, sitting down. "I'll walk you home," he said.

"If you want to. But you won't earn anything by it."

This irritated him slightly. "Maybe I wasn't trying to earn anything," he said.

She walked ahead of him when he stopped to pay the check and he noticed that she had a slight limp, her left foot hesitated gently against her stride. She kept her hands in her pockets. They walked in virtual silence, and when they came to her place—a faceless building in a long row of faceless buildings—she said "Thanks" and went inside before he had a chance even to attempt a foot in the door.

It took him a half hour of walking to find a liquor store. Before he found it he passed a poolroom, closed. He bought a fifth of Scotch, took it back to his hotel room with him and, before he went to bed, set it, unopened, on the green metal dresser.

8

HE AWOKE, sweating from the heat in his room, at seven-thirty that evening. After dressing, he went downstairs, out to the bus station, getting his suitcase from the locker but putting in another dime and leaving the pool cue. He would not be needing that for quite a while. It might be several weeks before he would want to advertise himself.

Before he left he looked, on a long-odds gamble, into the lunchroom. The girl was not there. Then he went back to his room, shaved, and changed his clothes. Coming out he left a bundle of dirty shirts with the woman in the lobby, telling her to send them out for him. He made a mental note to buy himself some new socks and underwear. He hadn't brought enough.

Then he went looking for a poolroom.

He found one on a street named Parmenter, a hole in the wall called Wilson's Recreation Hall, the kind of place with green paint on the windows. There were three beat-up pool tables, green-shaded incandescent lamps, and an old man to rack the balls. There were a bar and a back room—for booking race bets or for a card game. The door was open and he could see a round table and some chairs, but nobody was in the back room. Up front a small, indecently wrinkled man was sitting behind an ancient cash register that squatted, its sides decorated in phony rococo, on the bar. He looked up as Eddie came in.

It was a crummy place, a filthy, crooked-looking place, but Eddie felt at home in it. There were probably ten thousand poolrooms in the country, identical, down to the back room and the old man with the corrugated face, to Wilson's Recreation Hall on Parmenter Street in Chicago, and Eddie felt as if he had played in at least half of them.

There was one game going on. On the front table two men were playing one-pocket, a desultory, early-evening game of one-pocket. Eddie sat and watched them for almost an hour before one man quit and Eddie, grinning his very best, most personable grin, invited the remaining man to play for a while with him. Maybe for a half dollar on the side, just to pass the time . . .

And thus, easily, with hardly a second thought, Eddie Felson came full circle, starting where he had begun, scuffling, charming himself into a fifty-cent game of pool. He won seven dollars. He worked for that; spending three hours at it, in hope of getting the man to raise the bet, trying to prod him into playing for a dollar a game, or, with luck, two dollars. But the man quit and left him with seven dollars and in an empty poolroom. Eddie shrugged his shoulders. You have to start somewhere. . . .

He found a restaurant and ate a steak. Then he wandered in search of another poolroom. This one he found by recognizing the familiar dull crash of a rack of balls being broken open as he walked by it on the street. The place was on the third floor of a building, above a hardware store; and he would have missed the small BILLIARDS sign if it hadn't been for the sound of the balls.

He did not have to wait long before he got into a game of snooker with three petty tout types, at five cents a point. Snooker is a game played with small balls and on a table with very tight and bouncy pockets; it is impossible to play it in a fast, loose style—Eddie's style—the balls will not stay in the pockets unless they are shot with care and precision. It was not Eddie's kind of game, but the other players were so poor that he had to hold himself back in spite of this.

The other men were feeling good and Eddie mixed with them, buying a few rounds of drinks and telling an occasional joke. They seemed to think he was a great fellow. His feeling for them was not exactly contempt—although he knew they would have robbed him if they had a chance—but he found no remorse in taking them for forty dollars. It would have been more if the poolroom hadn't closed at two in the morning.

He figured his profit, after the drinks, at about thirty-two dollars. It would pay the rent; but he wasn't worried about the rent.

He was worried about at least a thousand dollars, which he needed very badly. He needed a thousand dollars so that he could get his little leather satchel out of the locker at the bus station and walk—no, take a taxicab—over to Bennington's Billiard Room and play straight pool with Minnesota Fats. Not with Jackie French or George the Fairy, but with Minnesota Fats, the fat man with the jerky chin, the little eyes, the rings, the ballet steps, the curly hair, and six thousand dollars of Eddie Felson's money. And all of Eddie Felson's pride.

Eddie put his cue stick in the rack. As he left, the proprietor said, "Come back, mister," but he did not reply to this. He figured that he would be back, however.

He was not accustomed to staying up all night; but he had got his hours badly twisted. He would have to get the landlady at the hotel to wake him earlier next time; maybe in three or four days he could get on some kind of reasonable schedule. He could start hustling around the rooms at noon, try and get to bed by three in the morning.

Also he would have to make some contacts, try finding ways of getting some bigger money; he would get nowhere by scuffling indefinitely. And once he got himself a reputation as a winner, in the circuit of local small poolrooms, winning even thirty or forty dollars would become hard to do. He could not go back to Bennington's, not without capital. Probably no one there would play him anyway, no one except Fats. They had already seen him play his best stick, knew what he could make happen on a pool table. He was not certain yet what he had already done, in the first, staggering game at Bennington's—but, whatever it was, he would have to make money. And, not only that, he would have to find some action, some important, high-money action. That was something he needed, in many ways.

For this night, now that the poolrooms were closed and there was nothing for him to do, he had already dimly formulated the framework of a plan involving something else that interested him: the girl. Thinking about her he had become aware of possibilities. He needed a girl, and he was beginning to feel that he needed this one.

Putting the plan into effect required first that he go to his room, clean himself up and change his clothes. He did this, and also straightened the room a little, smoothing out the half-made bed and filing some miscellaneous things away in a drawer of the bureau. He liked a room to be neat, in order. Then, leaving the fifth, he went out, bought a pint of Scotch, and slipped this into the breast pocket of his sport coat. There was a mirror in the liquor store and he examined himself in it. He looked good—neat and quietly dressed. Unlike a good many gamblers, Eddie liked dark colors, and he was wearing a dark gray coat, gray slacks, and plain black shoes. The only thing about him that could have said "Hustler" was the gray silk sport shirt, buttoned at the neck. He did not like the idea of carrying a bottle in his pocket—incredibly, he had never carried a bottle into a poolroom in his life—and he adjusted its weight so that it could not be noticed.

Outside it was becoming chilly. He walked briskly, with his hands in his pockets, until he came to the bus station. It was three o'clock. The lunchroom was roped off as before; there were two empty booths this time. The girl was not there. He sat down, ordered scrambled eggs and coffee. Immediately he began to feel foolish. What were the odds against the girl's coming in? It was too long a long shot. Maybe he should go by her place; he knew where it was. But what would he do when he got there? He didn't even know what apartment she lived in; and he didn't think she would take it very well even if he did know which door to knock on. But waiting in the bus station on the off-odds chance that she might come in was a stupid gamble.

But he didn't leave. He ate his eggs, and when he finished ordered another cup of coffee. He began smoking a cigarette.

At four-thirty he looked up and saw her coming in the door. She was wearing a heavy knit blue cardigan, with a big collar that came up to her ears. Her hands were jammed into her pockets; she looked sleepy. But one thing he noticed well; she was wearing more lipstick, and her hair was carefully combed. Somehow he felt nervous; she looked good.

For a moment he felt a tinge of panic. She would sit somewhere else and he would be left feeling like a fool. But she didn't. She came, limping over toward him, sat down, and said, "Hi."

"Hello," he said, and then grinned. The grin, this time, was not part of the hustle. He felt it. "Waiting for a bus?"

"That's right," she said, settling down into the seat, her hands still in her pockets as if she were badly chilled. "Leaves at six o'clock."

"Couldn't sleep?" he said.

"God no." She was becoming more expansive. "Did you ever wake up in an empty apartment at 4 A.M. and hear a Greyhound bus shifting gears outside your windows? Were you ever so wide awake that you thought you could never sleep again? Until you got out of bed, and felt like you were going to pass out?"

He grinned at her. "No."

She shrugged her shoulders. Then she said, "My name—you may not believe this—is Sarah."

"Eddie. What do you do for a living, Sarah?"

She laughed lightly. "By trade, I drink. Also a student, at the university. Economics. Six hours a week, Tuesdays and Thursdays."

That did not seem right. "College student" to him meant convertibles and girls with glasses. Nor did he think of college people sitting alone at night in places like this one. They were supposed to come in groups, singing, drinking beer—things like that.

"Why economics?" he said.

She smiled. "Who knows? To get a Master's degree maybe."

He wasn't sure what a Master's degree was; but it sounded impressive enough. The girl was obviously an egghead type, which was fine. He liked brains, and he admired people who read books. He had read a few himself. "You don't look like a college girl," he said.

"Thanks. College girls at the university never do. We're all emancipated types. Real emancipated."

"I don't mean that—whatever it means—I mean you don't look young enough."

"I'm not. I'm twenty-six. I had polio once, and missed five years of grade school."

Immediately he had an image of her as a little waxy girl on a poster, the kind of cardboard gimmick that sits by a collection jar on the counter of a poolroom, next to the razor blades.

"You mean braces and crutches and wheel chairs; all that?" His voice was not being particularly sympathetic; merely interested. Seeing her that way was like a look into a strange world he had heard of but never seen, had hardly felt existed save on the posters in drugstores and poolrooms. And once he had seen a movie trailer, where they had turned on the lights and tried to hustle him for his pocket change. He remembered wondering if the sick little kids in the movie knew they were being put on the make when the man had come around to take their pictures.

"Yes," she said, "all that. And books."

She was quiet for a moment, and then she said, "Look, let's have another cup of coffee. It's still an hour until six."

There it was, his opening. He suddenly felt nervous again, and cursed himself silently for feeling that way. "It doesn't have to be," he said.

She looked at him quizzically. Then she said, "I think I know what that means. Only I'm not going."

He tried to grin. "I didn't expect you to. I'm meeting you halfway. I've got a pint of Scotch in my pocket."

Her voice immediately became cold. "And you want me just to step out in the alley, is that it?"

"No," he said. "Hell, no. You know better than that. Right here."

She looked at him a moment, then shrugged her shoulders noncommittally. "Can this be done?" she said. "Legally?"

"I thought you were an old hand." He slipped the bottle out of his pocket, under his coat, down to the seat beside him. "This is done all the time." He grinned, "By the pros." He began cutting at the top with his thumbnail.

With the bottle open beside him and hidden by his coat, he told the waitress to bring them Cokes. Sarah made a wry face and, when the waitress was gone, said, "Scotch and Coca-Cola?"

"Just wait," he said. "We can beat that rap too."

When the Cokes came, in glasses, he told her to drink hers. "I detest Coca-Cola," she said.

"Drink it," he said. They drank them. Then he took her glass, empty except for the crushed ice, and asked her if she could drink it straight.

"If I have to," she said.

He filled her glass almost full with Scotch, then poured a little water in it from her water glass. "Here," he said, sliding it across the table to her. Then he began filling his own.

He had done this kind of thing before, with a gang from the poolroom; but it had always seemed a cheap thing to do—like the guffawing types who turn up half pints in the back seats of cars and then go out and pinch girls on the ass. But here, with Sarah, it did not seem that way.

At the first sip she grinned at him. "You're a great man, Eddie," she said. "You know how to beat the system."

They were working on their third one and the bottle was two-thirds empty when, abruptly, the waitress descended on them.

Her voice was high and cracked; she looked and sounded as if they had delivered her a gross personal insult. "You can't do that in *here,* mister." As if she were the whole Greyhound Lines herself. "This isn't that kind of place."

He looked up at her, trying to make his face serious and innocent. "How's that?"

"I said you can't sit in here and drink whiskey like you're doing." She peered at him nervously now. "I never saw the like."

"Okay," he said, "I'm sorry."

The woman's voice assumed a kind of wounded ferocity.

"You're gonna have to leave, mister. The both of you." It struck him that she had a hillbilly twang. This was amusing. "Or I'm gonna have to call a policeman in."

He got up, finishing his drink. "Sure," he said. "I'm sorry."

They went outside and stood on the sidewalk in the weak light and the cold air. The bottle was back in his pocket and he felt mildy drunk and sleepy. "Well," he said, "what next?"

She was huddled up in her sweater, standing close to him. The wind that was blowing was not summery, but cold. "What time is it?" Her voice was soft.

It was five-thirty, but he lied. "Five o'clock." His mind worked fast. There were several ways he could play this; he was not certain which would be the best. Maybe a long shot . . .

Gently, he slipped the bottle into her pocket. His hand brushed against hers, and he felt the brush of it all the way to his stomach. "Look," he said, "you better take this and go home to bed. You'll catch cold out here."

She looked up at him. Her eyes were wide. Then she looked away. "Thanks," she said, her voice very soft. She turned and began walking down the street, away from him. He watched her, watching the slight limp and the way her head was almost hidden by the big collar of her sweater. Her hands were still in her pockets, one now protectively over the bottle. Then, suddenly, she turned and began limping back, slowly. For a moment he felt as if he could not breathe.

When she came up she stood in front of him, solid and small, and looked up at him steadily. Her feet were planted slightly apart. Her eyes were very earnest and they looked his face over carefully. Then she said, "You just won, Eddie. Come on."

9

HER APARTMENT WAS ON THE FOURTH FLOOR; they had to walk up the stairs. They climbed them silently, and he said nothing when they went in, but seated himself on the sofa. She began taking off her sweater, and said, "I'll get a couple of glasses." She went into the kitchen. The blouse she was wearing was white, silky, and it clung loosely to her back.

The apartment was shabby, but there were some nice touches to it, and he noticed these. All the hotel rooms he had lived in during his ten years of hustling pool had made him more, rather than less, interested in the way a room was furnished. In front of him was a long low coffee table, its top of white marble, its legs of elaborate, filigreed brass. The walls were of gray, cracked plaster, but on one of them, over a painted brick fireplace with broken bricks, hung a huge picture in a white frame. The picture was of a sad-looking clown in a bright orange suit, holding a staff. Eddie looked at this carefully, not understanding what it meant, but liking it. The clown looked mean as a snake.

There was one big window, with white curtains edged with gold; and a cheap, painted bookcase in the same colors. Books were everywhere, in bright jackets—on the coffee table, in the seat of an armchair, stacked on what must have been a dining table. Around the edges of the rug the floor was painted with the ugly brown paint that people paint floors with. It reminded him of his mother's home in Oakland; linoleum and painted wood, and the refrigerator on the back porch.

Apparently, the place had three rooms. The big living room, the tiny kitchen in which Sarah was now fumbling with the ice cubes, and what was obviously a bedroom, its door half open, leading into the room he was in.

When she handed him his drink she looked at him and said, "Eddie, don't make a pass."

He did not answer but took the drink and began sipping it. Suddenly, he cursed himself silently; he had forgotten about the fifth at his hotel room. He would need it; the pint would soon be gone.

She was sitting now, watching him with a blank look, holding her knee, abstractedly rubbing the edge of the glass against the side of her neck. The light in the room seemed gray and her arms were white. There was a delicate and fine line of a blue vein in her wrist, branching gently on the white skin of her inner forearm. The skin at the side of her knees was white, too, smooth as if stretched taut, as if it would be resilient to the touch. Above her knee, below the edge of her skirt, was a fine line of white lace.

Well, here we go, he thought, *fast and loose.* He got up slowly, setting his drink down.

"Don't, Eddie," she said. "Not now."

The chair she was sitting in had broad arms. He sat on one of these, letting his arm fall across the back of the chair. He set his free hand on her shoulder, lightly. She turned her head down and away from him. "Eddie," she said, "I didn't mean this when I asked you to come up."

"Sure," he said, "I didn't either." Then he put the palm of his free hand against the side of her face, and bent down and kissed her on the mouth. Her cheek was warm against his hand and her hair brushed against his forehead, smelling of whiskey. Her lips were hard. She did not kiss him back. He pulled away from her awkwardly, immediately angry. Then he got up and stood for a moment, facing the kitchen, and finished his drink. He set the glass down, and turned to look at her. She was staring at her whiskey glass. He could not tell what her expression meant.

There was only one way to play it from here—and that was a long shot. He did not look at her again but walked out the door, hesitated, and began going down the stairs.

And then when he had come to the landing he heard her voice, calling softly, "Eddie," and he turned and walked slowly back up the steps. She met him inside the door, standing, her mouth slightly open, her hands at her sides. Her voice was soft, nervous. "You win again, Eddie."

He pushed the door shut behind him. Then he reached out

and put one hand behind her back, pressing gently against her silk blouse, his fingertips quivering slightly against invisible, taut straps. He cupped the other hand over her breast. Then he bent forward slowly, mouth open, into her warm, quick, shallow breath. Her mouth against his was like an electric current. It had been a long time. . . .

10

HER VOICE AWAKENED HIM, saying, "We have no eggs." He looked around, dazed. Red neon came in the window, dully. The sky was black, tinged with the lights. He could smell coffee. He rolled over; Sarah was gone from the bed. And then in a moment he saw her come padding, limping in from the kitchen, wearing a white flannel bathrobe and furry slippers, her eyes swollen from sleep. She stopped in the doorway a moment, then came and sat beside him on the bed. "We have no eggs," she said. "Do you have money?"

He reached out a hand and laid it on her arm. "Get in bed," he said.

She looked down at him with gravity. "I want breakfast," she said. "Where's your money?"

He rolled over. "In my pants pocket. Buy anything you want. Buy a coffee cake, the kind with pineapple on it."

"Okay," she said. He let himself fall back into sleep. . . .

She got him out of bed when she came back with the sack of groceries; he dressed while she was frying the eggs. He was sitting on the edge of the bed, putting his shoes on, feeling good, when she said from the other room, "What do you do, Eddie? For a living?"

He did not answer her for a minute. Then he said, "Does it make any difference?"

She didn't say anything further, but in a minute she was at the door, looking at him. "No," she said, and then, back in the kitchen, she laughed wryly, "I should be glad I've got a man."

The eggs were poorly cooked and the coffee was worse than restaurant coffee. The coffee cake was good. He was hungry and did away with it all. Then, when he finished, he looked at her and said, "I have to go out. Suppose I pick up some salami and come back in about four or five hours?"

"Sure," she said, "and bring some cheese."

He decided, suddenly, that there would be no use edging around with it. "I've got a suitcase. . . ."

She looked at him a moment and then shrugged, "Bring it. I expected you to."

It was so simple that it came as a shock. "I wasn't sure . . ." he said.

"Look," she smiled, "no strings—okay?"

He hesitated a moment, and then grinned at her. "Okay," he said.

In the morning she had to go to class, at ten o'clock. After fixing himself a cheese sandwich, he went back to bed and lay there thinking, first about himself and then, gradually, about the reason that he was in Chicago in the first place.

He thought about the profession of hustling pool, and about the men in it, feeling somehow that he must organize what he knew, must find out his position in the system, now that he was on his own and almost broke, in Chicago, in the summer. . . .

As Charlie had told him and as he had learned himself, in snatches—always, before, at a distance—there are two kinds of hustler, two kinds of gambler: the big-time and the small. Their sources of income are vastly different. The income of the big-time gambler is limited in range, although never in amount. And his expenses are high. The small-time men—the scufflers, musclers, dollar jumpers—prey in nibbles: on unwary but seldom wealthy drunks; schoolboys who aspire to what they take to be manhood; middle-aged men who aspire to what they take to be youthfulness; and the smaller scufflers, musclers and dollar jumpers. They live the obsequious, frustrating life once allotted to the petty courtier, now seen in its purest form in the two-dollar tout and the professional drink cadger. Such men occasionally engage in small con games—although seldom; all con men gamble, but few gamblers con—or they attempt to ride on the great money bus, Sex; usually trying for the taillights or bumper, through part-time pimping, the sale of various obscene artifacts, even through gigolo work, all of which are professions grossly underpaid.

Some of this small-time money—the greasy money—is filtered up to the big-time gamblers, the true professional men;

but only—as Eddie was beginning to find out—seldom, and then in small amounts. The main sources of the big-timer—like Minnesota Fats—are only three: the well-to-do sportsman, the big con man, and the other big-timer. The well-to-do sportsman comes in two breeds: the tweedy philosopher with a gun collection and money, and the Miami Beach industrialist, with friends in the Senate and money. The big con man is hard to recognize, except that he is always personable and intelligent; but when he has money he has plenty, and he likes to lose it. And the other big-timer is somebody you don't seek out when all you need is money. Games between full-scale, professional gamblers always have things at stake which are not as easily negotiable or recognizable as cash. It's said that when whales fight whales it is never merely because one is hungry. And that makes sense; the sea is very full of smaller fish.

But these factors were working against Eddie, who, by nature, by skill, by ambition, by everything except income and experience, was a big-timer; and who was beginning to feel that he must have a thousand dollars before he was anything at all. In the first place it was summer. Wealthy sportsmen are seldom in the big northern cities in the summer; they are sunning or shading themselves in places created especially for wealthy sportsmen. And the con men are with the wealthy sportsmen, usually buying them drinks. Most of the big-timers are following the races—horse, boat, automobile—or the sportsman and the big con. (This makes a sort of procession: sportsman, con, gambler; with money in the lead, as is only fitting and proper.) True, some big gamblers remain behind, like Minnesota Fats. Either they have business connections at home, or they do not find it necessary to leave town in order to find action. A man like Minnesota Fats needs no agent; he attracts—as Eddie knew well—his own clientele.

Summer was against him, in Chicago. Also against him was the fact that now he had announced his presence in town and his high talents so clearly, in the one big game, it would be impossible for him to enter any major poolroom—any big-timers' room—without being spotted. He would go back to Bennington's; but not until he had money. And he had been depending on a manager, Charlie, for too long. Without Charlie his only hustle was to talk himself into a game and squeeze out what he could. He was good at the talking in part—was, in fact, phenomenal—but found the squeezing difficult. He had lost some of the touch—and all of the enthusiasm—for it. . . .

After Sarah had come back from school and had taken him to bed, they talked, lying together, barely touching. He did not tell her much about himself, did not feel that he had to. He told her that his father was an electrician, his mother dead, that for a long time he had made his living "one way or another." She asked him what that meant, but he did not answer her. He did not want to say, "I'm a pool hustler. I intend to be the best goddamn pool hustler in the business," so he said nothing.

Her father and mother had been divorced for a long time. Her father, a moderately wealthy man, a car dealer of some kind, was remarried and living in St. Louis, where she had been raised and had gone to school. The first of every month she got a check for three hundred dollars from him.

Her mother lived in Toledo; they had not seen each other for five years. She spoke several times of herself as an alcoholic and as if they, she and Eddie, had some kind of contract of depravity between them. He did not like this; it was phony and mildly embarrassing. But, if she liked to think of herself that way, as harder, more dissolute than she actually was, it did not really make much difference. Maybe she would outgrow it. Maybe the kind of treatment that he was giving her would make for a change.

When he left the apartment he walked for a while, not heading for any particular place, but wanting to walk and to think.

Finally he came to the poolroom where he had won the forty dollars at snooker. He did not like the place; its walls were too bright, with glaring white tile like a subway station and bright incandescent lamps; but he had done well there before.

He did not do well this time. There was nothing happening, nothing at all. But then, he had something to go home to. . . .

He did not often think of Minnesota Fats and of the game they had played, not explicitly; but he would think around the edges of it—the whole forty hours of it were now compressed in his mind into a single event, as if it had all happened in an instant, so that the memory was a kaleidoscopic picture of the fat man with the rings on his fingers and of the moment when the high ceiling of Bennington's had spun, slid, and fallen on him, and of himself lying on the floor with the sound of the cue ball crashing in his dulled ears and his money and his victory gone. And, without detailing the events in sequence, his mind could skirt around the whole thing, licking at its edges, probing at it, wanting to twist it, ease it, pull it, jerk it out, as the restless tongue probes at a strand of food wedged between the teeth; or the fingers, working of their own volition, toy with the scab that overlays a cut.

And there was beginning to be a feeling of restlessness, the unformulated knowledge that he must be setting about his business, that there were things he had to do. There was money to be won, capital to be earned. And there was the need for practice. . . .

It was several days later that he got into a poker game, got into it because he was becoming desperate for action. It seemed impossible to locate a pool game that had any chance of becoming worth while.

It was in the middle of an afternoon. He was in the little poolroom near the Loop, on Parmenter Street, trying to find some kind of game, any game at all. There was nothing doing, nothing whatever. There were only four men in the pool-playing part of the place, and all of them knew him. He offered to play one of them a handicap game where he would shoot with one hand in his pocket—jack-up pool—while the other man shot the usual way. The man laughed, pleasantly enough, and shook his head. "You're outta my league, mister."

The door to the back room was open and Eddie wandered back, not thinking of anything in particular, feeling disgusted with himself, irritated. He felt, for a minute, like giving the whole thing up for the day and going back to Sarah's apartment and drinking with her. But there was something about that idea that made him uneasy. He looked around the room he was in, it was the first time he had been back there. Five men were sitting around a circular table covered with the faded green felt that could only have been a worn-out pool cloth, quietly playing cards. There were no other chairs in the room. He put his hands in his pockets and leaned against the wall.

The other men seemed hardly to notice his presence, and he watched them idly. It did not seem to be a very interesting game. The limit was fifty cents; and the bets were not running very high or very fast. But one of the men in the game caught Eddie's attention. There was something vaguely familiar about his face—although it was a totally unremarkable face—and the way he played poker seemed interesting. One man in the game was drinking whiskey from a highball glass; two had coffee cups in front of them; but this man had a glass of milk on the table, and he would sip from it carefully after every hand. Also, although he did nothing sensational, he seemed to be quietly winning; and the other men, very terse with one another, spoke to him with respect. They called him Bert.

He sat upright, straight in his chair, a fairly small man of normal build, maybe a little heavy around the waist, although that appearance could have been caused by his sitting. His features were regular, slightly womanish if anything, for his skin was fair, and his cheeks mildly pink. His hair was brown, very fine, and freshly trimmed. He wore steel-rimmed glasses. There was something prim about him, about the set of his pale, thin mouth and the careful, almost prissy, way he handled the cards. And, although the face was ordinary, there was something very odd about it that puzzled Eddie until he realized that Bert's hair was so fine that he seemed not to have eyebrows.

He had not intended to get in the game—he knew very little about poker—but when one of the players quit, complaining that he had to meet his wife, Eddie found himself slipping into the empty chair and calmly asking for chips. He immediately found himself in possession of the first two winning hands: two little pairs followed by an eight-high straight. For a moment he suspected a hustle; but he knew enough about poker to be able to discount that after a few minutes' careful watching; and he quickly became wrapped up in the game, enjoying what was his first action in several days. But he played wildly, lost a few critical hands, and, when the game broke up at supper-time—it seemed to be an extraordinarily casual game compared with the poker he had known before—he had lost twenty dollars, which he could not afford. Bert, who had been quiet and meticulous throughout, had won about forty or fifty, as well as Eddie could estimate, since he had started playing.

The other men left the poolroom, but Bert went into the front and seated himself at the bar, and when Eddie started to leave—the pool tables were now empty—he said, affably, "Have a drink?"

Eddie felt a little irritation in his voice. "I thought you only drank milk."

Bert pursed his lips. Then he smiled. "Only when I'm working." He made what seemed for him an ambitious gesture, making his voice friendly. "Sit down. I owe you a drink anyway."

Eddie sat down on a stool beside him. "What makes you owe me a drink?"

Bert peered at him through the glasses, inquiringly. It struck Eddie that probably he was near-sighted. "I'll tell you about it sometime," he said.

Irritated by this, Eddie changed the subject. "So why drink milk?"

Bert asked the bartender for two whiskies, specifying a brand, the kind of glass, and the number of ice cubes, without consulting Eddie. Then he peered at him again, apparently to give thought, now that *that* was taken care of, to his question. "I like milk," he said. "It's good for you." The bartender set glasses in front of them on the bar and dropped in ice cubes. "Also, if you make money gambling, you keep a clear head." He looked at Eddie intently. "You start drinking whiskey gambling and it gives you an excuse for losing. That's something you don't need, an excuse for losing."

There was something cranky, fanatical, about the serious, lip-pursing way that Bert spoke, and it made Eddie uneasy. The words, he knew, were directed at him; but he did not like the sound of them and he did not let himself reach for their meaning. The bartender had finished with the drinks and Bert paid for them—giving the exact change. Eddie lifted his and said, "Cheers." Bert said nothing and they both sipped silently for a few minutes. The bartender—the old, wrinkled man who was also rackboy, bookmaker and manager—went back to his chair and his reveries, whatever they were. There was no one else in the place. Some broad puffs of hot air came from the open doorway, but little else; nothing seemed to be going on in the street. A cop ambled by the door, lost in thought. Eddie looked at his wrist watch. Seven o'clock. Would Sarah feel like eating now? Probably not.

He looked at Bert and, abruptly, remembered the question that had been on his mind, hazily, all afternoon. "Where have I seen you before?" he asked.

Bert went on sipping his drink, not looking at him. "At Bennington's. The time you hooked Minnesota Fats and threw him away."

That was it, of course. He must have been one of the faces in the crowd. "You a friend of Minnesota Fats?" Eddie said it a little contemptuously.

"In a way." Bert smiled faintly, as if pleased with himself for some obscure reason. "You might say we went to school together."

"He's a poker player too?"

"Not exactly." Bert looked at him, still smiling. "But he knows how to win. He's a real winner."

"Look," Eddie said, suddenly angry, "so I'm a loser; is that it? You can quit talking like Charlie Chan; you want to laugh at me, that's your privilege. Go ahead and laugh." He did not like this leaving-the-fact-unnamed kind of talk. But hadn't he been thinking that way himself, for a week or more—leaving the fact unnamed? But what was the fact, the one he wasn't naming? He finished his drink quickly, ordered another.

Bert said, "That isn't what I meant. What I meant was, that was the first time in ten years Minnesota Fats' been hooked. Really hooked."

The thought pacified Eddie considerably. It pleased him; maybe he had scored some sort of victory after all. "That a fact?" he said.

"That's a fact." Bert seemed to be loosening up. He had ordered another whiskey and was starting on it. "You had him hooked. Before you lost your head."

"I got drunk."

Bert looked incredulous. Then he laughed—or, rather,

chuckled—softly. "Sure," he said, "you got drunk. You got the best excuse in the world for losing. It's no trouble at all, losing. When you got a good excuse."

Eddie looked at him, levelly. "That's a lot of crap."

Bert ignored this. "You lost your head and grabbed the easy way out. I bet you had fun, losing your head. It's always nice to feel the risks fall off your back. And winning; that can be heavy on your back, too, like a monkey. You drop that load, too, when you find yourself an excuse. Then, afterward, all you got to do is learn to feel sorry for yourself—and lots of people learn to get their kicks that way. It's one of the best indoor sports, feeling sorry." Bert's face broke into an active grin. "A sport enjoyed by all. Especially the born losers."

It did not make very much sense; but it made enough, dimly, to make him angry again, even though the whiskey was now filtering through his empty stomach, placating him, busily solving his problems—the old ones and the ones yet to come. "I made a mistake. I got drunk."

"You got more than drunk. You lost your head." Bert was pushing now, in a kind of delicate, controlled way. "Some people lose their heads cold sober. Cards, dice, pool; it makes no difference. You want to make a living that way, you want to be a winner, you got to keep your head. And you got to remember that there's a loser somewhere in you, whining at you, and you got to learn to cut his water off. Otherwise you better get a steady job."

"Okay," Eddie said. "Okay. You win. I'll think about it." He did not intend to think about it; he wanted to shut Bert up, vaguely aware that the man, ordinarily quiet, was loosening himself from some kind of tension, some kind of personal fight of his own, was sticking pins into him, Eddie, to drive out his own private devil. And he had thought about it enough already.

Bert had finished his second drink and was saying, "So what do you do now?"

"What do you think? I hustle up enough capital so I can play him again. And this time I leave the bottle and concentrate on what I'm doing."

Bert peered at him, not smiling this time. "There's plenty of other ways to lose. You can find one easy."

"What if I'm not looking?"

"You will be. Probably." Bert waved—an incomplete, supercilious wave—at the bartender, signaling for another. "I don't think you'll be ready to play Fats again for ten years." His voice sounded prissy, smug, as he said it.

Eddie looked at him, astonished. "What do you mean, ten years? You saw me hook him before."

"And I saw you let him go too."

"Sure. And I learned something. I'll know better next time."

"You probably won't. And you think Fats didn't learn something too?"

Somehow, he hadn't thought of that one before. "Okay. Maybe he did." The bartender was pouring another drink. Eddie took out a cigarette, offered one to Bert. Bert shook his head. "And maybe he learned the wrong things. Maybe he thinks the next time I play him I'll get drunk again and throw away the game. Maybe I wanted him to learn that." That was a fantastic lie, and he realized it even as he said it.

Bert's look became mildly contemptuous. "If you think that's right you'll never learn a thing. How many times do I have to say it, it wasn't the whiskey that beat you? I know it, you know it, Fats knows it."

Eddie knew now, what he meant; but he persisted in not understanding him. "You think he shoots better than I do, is that it? You got a right to think that."

Bert had got a pack of potato chips from a rack on the counter. He chewed on one of these, nibbling at it thoughtfully, like a careful, self-conscious mouse. Eddie noticed that his teeth were very even, bright, like a movie star's. Then Bert said, "Eddie, I don't think there's a pool player living that shoots better straight pool than I saw you shoot last week at Bennington's." He pushed the rest of the potato chip past his thin lips, into the pretty teeth. "You got a talent."

This was pleasant to hear, even in its context. Eddie had hardly been aware of how impoverished his vanity was. But he tried to make his tone of voice wry. "So I got a talent," he said. "Then what beat me?"

Bert pulled another potato chip from the bag, offered him one, and then said, his voice now offhand, casual, "Character."

Eddie laughed lightly. "Sure," he said. "Sure."

Bert's voice suddenly returned to its prissy, schoolteacherish tone. "You're goddamn right I'm sure. Everybody's got talent. I got talent. But you think you can play big money straight pool—or poker—for forty straight hours on nothing but talent?" He leaned toward Eddie, peering at him again, nearsightedly, through the thick, steel-rimmed glasses. "You think they call Minnesota Fats the Best in the Country just because he's got talent? Or because he can do trick shots?" He pulled back from Eddie and took his drink in hand, looking now very pompous. “Minnesota Fats,” he said, “has got more character in one finger than you got in your whole goddamn skinny body.” Bert looked away from him. “He drank as much whiskey as you did.”

The truth of what Bert was saying was so forceful that it took Eddie a moment to drive it from his mind, to explain it away. But even this was hard to do, for Eddie had a kind of hard, central core of honesty that was difficult for him to deal with sometimes—a kind of embarrassing awareness that only a few people are afflicted with. But he managed to avoid the fact, to avoid capitulation to what Bert was saying, that he, Eddie, was—simply enough—not man enough to beat a man like Fats. But, not knowing what else to say, he said, aware that it was feeble, “Maybe Fats knows *how* to drink.”

Bert would not let him go now, knew that he had him. Eddie became abruptly aware that Bert talked like he played poker, with a kind of quiet, strong—very strong—pushing. “You're goddamn right he knows how,” Bert said softly. “And you think that's a talent too? Knowing how to drink whiskey? You think Minnesota Fats was born knowing how to drink?”

“Okay. Okay.” What did Bert want him to do? Prostrate himself on the floor? “So what do I do now? Go home?”

And Bert seemed to relax, knowing he had scored, had pushed his way through Eddie's consciousness and through his defenses—although Eddie still only partly understood all of what Bert had said, and was already prepared to rationalize the truth out of what he did understand. But Bert had suddenly quit pushing, and seemed now to be merely relaxing with his drink. “That's your problem,” he said.

"Then I'll stay here." For the first time in several hours Eddie grinned. The conversation seemed to have become normal now, the usual kind of understandable conversation, where the challenges are so deeply hidden or buried that you only accept them when you feel like taking a challenge, and then only to the degree that you choose. Eddie liked things to be that way. "I'll stay until I hustle up enough to play Minnesota Fats again. Maybe by then I'll develop myself some character."

Bert's voice was amused, but not pushing. "Maybe by then you'll die of old age." He paused. "How much do you think you're gonna need?"

"A thousand. Maybe more."

Bert set his drink down. "No. Three thousand at least. He'll start you out at five hundred a game. His tone was analytical now, detached and speculative. "And he's gonna beat your ass at first, because that's the way he plays when he comes up against a man who already knows the way the game is. He'll beat you flat, four or five games. Maybe more, depending on how steady your nerve is." He hesitated, "And he might—he just might—be a little scared of you. And that could change things. But I wouldn't count on it." He began chewing another potato chip. "And, either way, he'll beat your ass at first."

"How do you know? Nobody knows that much." There was something preposterous about this little prissy god sitting beside him, passing judgment on him, now affably and dispassionately. "I might beat him the first five games."

"Sure you might. But you won't. And how do I know?" Bert raised a finger significantly and pointed toward the door. Eddie turned, looking out. "See that Imperial out there? That's mine." Parked across the street was a long, new-looking black car, with large white-wall tires. "I like that car and I get a new one every year because I make it my business to know what people like Minnesota Fats—or like you—are gonna do." Then he smiled, with an afterthought. "And if I hadn't already paid for it I could of with the money I won in side bets. When you two were playing last week."

For a moment Eddie felt himself angry, remembering now for the first time the neat little man who was taking bets while the games were starting. Then he grinned, sipping his drink. "I guess you owe me these drinks after all."

"I told you I did." Bert gave his rare grin again. And, with the whiskey, Eddie began to feel a pleasant sense about Bert. Bert was smart; he knew the answers. Now he was saying, "And maybe I can help you out," almost as if he had at the same time begun to feel friendly. "With that three thousand."

But Eddie hesitated. Maybe there was an angle. "Why?" he said.

"Ten reasons. Maybe fifteen." He smiled, "Also, there's something in it for me."

Eddie grinned back at him. "That's what I figured. Go ahead."

"Well," Bert said, "I've been thinking about a game for you. A little game of pool, with a man named Findlay . . ."

Eddie had the bartender give him two hard-boiled eggs on a dish with some soda crackers. He peeled the eggs, made a little white mount of salt on the plate and began eating, while Bert told him about James Findlay, in carefully phrased detail. Findlay lived in Kentucky, in Lexington, and had a fame that was becoming wide-spread in gambling circles. Once a poker player notorious for his ability to lose, he had recently turned to pool, at which he was even more of a born loser. James, it seemed, was very rich; he owned twenty per cent of a tobacco company, through the graces of God and a dead aunt. He also owned a large house, and in the basement of this house he had a pool table. He seemed to enjoy thinking of himself as a hustler, a quaint aristocrat who took on all the passing hustlers in the genteel quiet of his own basement, while he smoked cork-tipped cigarettes and drank eight-year-old bourbon and invariably lost his ass. Fortunately, he apparently never kept books. And, fortunately for himself, he seldom let himself lose more than a few thousand. Also, he was a reasonably good player; it took a certain amount of skill to beat him—more skill than that of the average second-rate hustler. And he played no one but the best. Eddie found all of this interesting; Bert told it well and with the evident relish of a born arranger, a matchmaker.

After Bert was finished and Eddie had eaten the eggs, Eddie said, "How do we get to Lexington?"

"In my car."

"Fair enough." It would certainly be an improvement over the old Packard—although he would have preferred traveling with Charlie. "What's your percentage?"

Bert blinked at him. "Seventy-five."

Eddie set down the napkin he had been wiping his mouth with. "What did you say?"

"Seventy-five. I get seventy-five per cent. You get twenty-five."

That was impossible. Fifty-fifty maybe, at the most . . .

"What do you . . . Who do you think you are, General Motors? That's a very large slice."

Bert's smile vanished abruptly. "What do you mean, a large slice? What kind of odds do you think are right for these days anyway? I'm touting you on this game; that's worth ten per cent anywhere by itself. I'm putting up the paper. I'm supplying transportation. And I'm putting up my time, which isn't exactly worthless. For this I get a seventy-five per cent return on my money. If you win."

Eddie looked at him scornfully. "You think I can lose?"

Bert's voice was calm. "I never saw you do anything else."

"You saw me beat Minnesota Fats for eighteen thousand."

There was irritation in Bert's voice again. "Look," he said, "you want to hustle pool, don't you? This game isn't like football. Nobody pays you for yardage. When you hustle you keep score real simple. After the game is over you count your money. That's the way you find out who was best. The only way."

"Okay," Eddie said, "Then why back me at all? Back yourself. Find you a big, fat poker game and get rich. You know all the angles."

Bert smiled again. "I'm already rich, I told you. And poker happens to be slow these days."

"You probably picked up fifty this afternoon."

"That's business. I want action. And one thing I think you're good for is action. Besides, like I say, you got talent."

"Thanks."

"So we go to Lexington?"

Eddie looked at him. It occurred to him that Bert had probably been working up to this since he had first offered to buy him a drink. "We don't."

Bert shrugged his shoulders. "Suit yourself."

"I will. Maybe if you cut that slice down to bite size we might talk some more."

"Then we won't talk. I don't make bad bets."

Eddie started to get up. "Thanks for the drinks," he said.

"Wait a minute." Bert looked at him, standing now. "What are you gonna do about that money?"

"I'll scuffle around. Somebody told me about a room called Arthur's where there's action."

Bert looked concerned. "Stay out of that place," he said. "It's not your kind of room. They'll eat you alive."

Eddie grinned down at him. Bert seemed very small from where he was standing, next to him and over him. "When did you adopt me?" he said.

Bert looked back at him, peering at him closely again, through the thick glasses. "I don't know when it was," he said, quietly.

11

HE DID NOT GO TO SARAH'S APARTMENT, but to another bar, a place where there was a great deal of noise and some kind of unfathomable gambling game, a game where a girl sat in a high chair and shook out dice from a cup while a group of men stood around her making bets for drinks and noisily losing, all of it under the shrill overlay of a persistent, grinding jukebox. And then, on his second drink, he realized abruptly that this wasn't doing any good, that it never had and never would—not for him. He would have to find something else, something to break him out of the trap that this city of Chicago had laid for him, the trap that had already twisted—not killed, but twisted—his confidence, and that was already making him a whining, two-dollar scuffler. Or that would make him an employee, somebody else's man. He paid for his drink and left. It seemed to take a long while to walk out of range of the jukebox; and even when he could no longer hear it, its loud insistence still rung, an imbecilic, thumping melody, in his head.

He walked to the bus station where he had left his cue. He did not think it out, but this seemed to be the best thing to do, the only step he could make in the direction he wanted to go.

He had the key in his pocket, found the right locker and took the round case from it. And instantly he felt foolish, standing there in the bus station holding a pool cue in a satchel. What was he going to do? Go to Bennington's, beat on the desk, shout for Minnesota Fats, find him, and start a game of pool? With two hundred dollars?

He was more drunk on the whiskey he'd had than he realized. He bumped into an old woman as he was going out the door, a ragged, shriveled woman with a copy of *Photoplay* under her arm. She glared at him. He scowled, pushed by her and went out the door.

He walked the three blocks to Sarah's, hands stuffed in his coat pockets, the cue stick under his arm, his silk shirt open at the collar, listening to the sound of his leather heels hitting the concrete, letting them hit it hard, as if he were trying to drive something out of himself. It was not Bert, he was aware of that, although Bert was part of it, part of the cat and mouse. But Bert was not a blood-thirsty cat but a reasonable, reasonably greedy one. Nor, even, was it Minnesota Fats, not entirely; for Fats was only an accessory to, a witness of, his humiliation. But he had won so much money, had been so high, and had never touched Fats. Had never shaken him, moved him, pushed him, had never altered the quiet and quick look of his little eyes, almost hidden by the enormous face. And something had happened to him, Eddie, something deep and shameful and hidden. What then? Why did he not want to think about Minnesota Fats, about the night at Bennington's—why not think about it? It was supposed to help to think about things like that, supposed to keep you from making the same mistake twice.

He would think about Bert. Bert was an interesting man. Bert had said something about the way a gambler wants to lose. That did not make sense. Anyway, he did not want to think about it. It was dark now, but the air was still hot. He realized that he was sweating, forced himself to slow down the walking. Some children were playing a game with a ball, in the street, hitting it against the side of a building. He wanted to see Sarah.

When he came in, she was reading a book, a tumbler of dark whiskey beside her on the end table. She did not seem to see him and he sat down before he spoke, looking at her and, at first, hardly seeing her. The room was hot; she had opened the windows, but the air was still. The street noises from outside seemed almost to be in the room with them, as if the shifting of gears were being done in the closet, the children playing in the bathroom. The only light in the room was from the lamp over the couch where she was reading.

He looked at her face. She was very drunk. Her eyes were swollen, pink at the corners. "What's the book?" he said, trying to make his voice conversational. But it sounded loud in the room, and hard.

She blinked up at him, smiled sleepily, and said nothing.

"What's the book?" His voice had an edge now.

"Oh," she said. "It's Kierkegaard. Søren Kierkegaard." She pushed her legs out straight on the couch, stretching her feet.

Her skirt fell back a few inches from her knees. He looked away.

"What's that?" he said.

"Well, I don't exactly know, myself." Her voice was soft and thick.

He turned his face away from her again, not knowing what he was angry with. "What does that mean, you don't know, yourself?"

She blinked at him. "It means, Eddie, that I don't exactly know what the book is about. Somebody told me to read it, once, and that's what I'm doing. Reading it."

He looked at her, tried to grin at her—the old, meaningless, automatic grin, the grin that made everybody like him—but he could not. "That's great," he said, and it came out with more irritation than he had intended.

She closed the book, tucked it beside her on the couch. She folded her arms around her, hugging herself, smiling at him. "I guess this isn't your night, Eddie. Why don't we have a drink?"

"No." He did not like that, did not want her being nice to him, forgiving. Nor did he want a drink.

Her smile, her drunk, amused smile, did not change. "Then let's talk about something else," she said. "What about that case you have? What's in it?" Her voice was not prying, only friendly. "Pencils?"

"That's it," he said. "Pencils."

She raised her eyebrows slightly. Her voice seemed thick. "What's in it, Eddie?"

"Figure it out yourself." He tossed the case on the couch. She picked it up, fumbling with and then opening the buckle at the top. When she pulled out the silk-wound butt end she said, "Interesting," and then pulled out the other, thinner piece. "How do you work it?"

"It screws together."

She looked at it with frowning concentration for a moment, then deftly—in spite of her drunkenness—put the pieces in place and twisted them together. She ran her hand lightly over the silken end, holding the cue in her lap. Suddenly she said, raising her eyes, puzzled, "It's a pool stick!"

"That's right."

"It's like a fancy cane. All these inlays . . ." Then it seemed to hit her and she said, "Are you a pool shark, Eddie?"

He had never liked that term, and he did not like her tone of voice. "I play pool for money," he said.

She took a gulp of her drink, shuddered under it, and then laughed self-consciously. "I thought you were a salesman. Or maybe a confidence man . . ." She smiled at him. "I don't know. It seems strange. . . ."

He looked at her a minute, carefully, before he spoke. Then he said, "Why?"

She looked back to the cue in her lap. "I never knew a pool shark before. I thought they all wore double-breasted suits and striped shirts. . . ."

He started to answer this, but did not. She bit on her fingernail for a moment, and then said, "Why play pool?"

He had heard this before, several times. And always from women. "Why not?"

She was trying to sound serious, but her voice was still drunken. "You know what I mean. Do you make a living at it?"

"Sometimes. I'll do better."

This seemed to exasperate her. "But why *pool?* Couldn't you do something else?"

"Like what?" He noticed for the first time that she had light freckles at her elbows, and this discovery irritated him vaguely.

"Don't be cute about it," she said. "You know what I'm driving at. You could . . . sell insurance, something like that."

He looked at her for a moment, wondering whether he should take her to bed, work up a little action. "No," he said. "What I do I like fine."

He decided that it wouldn't be worth the effort. He stood up from the couch, stretched, and then went into the bedroom to the dresser mirror and began combing his hair. The mirror, like the clown in the living room, had a white frame. He combed his hair carefully, patting it on the left side and then patting down the slight wave. He needed a haircut. Which was always a nuisance.

Sarah spoke to him from the chair in the living room. "I've heard that pool can be a dirty game," she said.

He put the comb back in his pocket. "People say that," he said. "I've heard people say that myself."

"You're being comical," she said, trying to make her voice sound dry. And then, "*Is* it dirty?"

He walked back into the living room and, not looking at Sarah, looked instead at the clown. The clown looked back, sad and mean, holding the wooden staff. His fingers were painted in only sketchily, but they were graceful and sure of themselves. The clown was, apparently, unhappy, but was not to be pushed around; a good, solid clown and a figure to be respected. Eddie stretched again, his back to Sarah, still looking at the picture.

"Yes. It's dirty." He felt of his face, which needed a shave. "Anyway you look at it, it's dirty."

Then he walked into the bathroom and began undressing, hanging his clothes over the edge of the bathtub. On the back of the toilet Sarah kept a turtle in a glass bowl. At present, it was probably asleep. Eddie did not investigate this; but he thought about the turtle. A self-contained, cautious, withdrawn creature. Solid and reliable, like Bert—withdrawn, now, into its two houses: one given it by God, the other by the five-and-ten. The turtle asked no questions, and was required to give no answers.

Eddie put his pajamas on and went to bed. Before he turned the bedroom lights out, he saw that Sarah was still in the living room, staring at the wall. He rolled over and fell immediately asleep.

12

THE RIDE WAS A LONG ONE. The cab took him through a district of warehouses, of loud, dirty kids in the streets, of oculists and liquor stores and lady fortune tellers. The wooden building with the faded sign that said ARTHUR's was in the middle of a block, with a decaying heap of a warehouse on one side and a vacant lot on the other. It was early Saturday night and through the open window of the cab he could hear loud talk and hillbilly music coming from the bar. An ancient and greatly stooped man was shuffling down the street, near the sidewalk, muttering loudly to himself.

Eddie almost told the driver to take him back; he did not know this kind of place and it made him uneasy to be in it. But he needed money and he needed action and he got out of the cab. There was no movement of air and the air itself was very warm, tinged faintly with the smell of garbage. The door of the poolroom was open, and the clicking sounds of the balls seemed louder, out in the street, than he was used to hearing them sound inside.

Inside, the poolroom was very small, hot, smelling of creosote and, faintly, of stale urine. In the middle of the room was a large overhead fan with flat, black blades. From the center of this hung a curled streamer of flypaper, dotted with black. There was a cuspidor by each wall, sitting on the plank floor, and by each of these was a cluster of empty bottles—whiskey, Coca-Cola, and 7-Up.

Five men were playing nine ball on the front table. Besides the rack man, with the triangle hanging in the crook of his arm, there was only one spectator, a heavy, porcine man with a crushed felt hat, its brim turned up and fastened in front with a safety pin. Over the table two bare incandescent bulbs hung on frayed cords from the ceiling. They trembled with the vibration from the fan. Tied between the cords was a smudged cardboard sign that read OPEN GAME; and below this someone had written in pencil, PLAY AT YOUR OWN RISK.

The men were wearing overalls or khaki pants and either white T-shirts or the kind of slick-surfaced sport shirt that is translucent, outlining the underwear beneath it. There was one thin-faced young man—a man of about Eddie's age—whose face was pale and who, in spite of the khaki pants and sport shirt, had a dapper, sharp-eyed look—the B-movie version of the hustler: the pool shark.

He leaned against the wall and watched several games. No one seemed to notice him—the men were very intent with playing—and he was glad he had made a point of not wearing a coat. The pale young man seemed to be doing most of the winning. His style looked good, and he had a nice way of making the money balls, which he did so well that the other players called him "lucky"—for a good hustler the finest of compliments. Once, when the kid made what seemed a too obvious combination bank on the nine, Eddie looked closely at the face of the big man with the safety-pin hat—the others had called him Turtle—but the broad face showed no surprise or awareness when one of the men said, "You lucky punk," to the kid.

They were playing two dollars on the nine and a dollar on the five. A respectable game; you could win twelve dollars in maybe two or three minutes. The table was small—a four by eight—and had drop pockets, the kind that have been filed down to make the balls fall in easier. It would have been a lock table for any first-rate nine-ball player, a table a good man would have to try hard to miss on. Eddie's fingers began itching for a cue.

But he did not even have to invite himself in. After about twenty minutes a player quit and the kid looked at Eddie insolently and said, "You want in, friend?"

Eddie looked at him. He had always hated this kind: the sharp kind, the snotty, second-rate punk hustler. "Well," Eddie said, grinning at him, "maybe I'll try a couple for kicks."

"Sure thing, friend." One side of the kid's mouth drooped into a practiced casualness, the kind of thing picked up from pictures of hillbilly singers, practically a sneer. "Just watch who you're kicking."

The big man, who was now the game's only watcher, guffawed.

Eddie remained grinning. "I always watch who I'm kicking. Helps my aim." The big man did not laugh at this.

Eddie picked a cue out of the rack and began playing, using

the awkward style that Charlie had rehearsed him in years before, playing it especially carefully this time. He had to fool the kid, because the kid was the one with the money. And to fool another hustler is not always easy. So he played poorly, but managed to make the right shot at the right time every now and then, often enough to stay even with the game. He kept his eye on the kid, who seemed to suspect nothing.

And then, after about an hour, he began acting as if he were getting hot, sweating a little, acting high and strutting—another thing that Charlie had taught him—making enough wild shots to start winning in earnest, but missing enough to make it look convincing. And the kid did as Eddie hoped, making good shots, running balls without trying so much to appear lucky, drilling the money balls in with malice and skill. He always seemed to sneer at the nine ball before he made it, as if to convince himself of his power over it. In another hour they had driven the other men, grumbling, out of the game. Eddie was about sixty dollars ahead; the kid must have won more than that, for he had continued to collect quite often. Once, when he had lost and paid off to the kid, the other man leered at him and said, "That's tough, friend," and Eddie thought, *You just wait, you son of a bitch,* grinning at him.

Now, when the last other player had quit and they were all standing by the big man, watching the two of them, the kid gave him the same look and said, "It's you and me, friend."

"Say, that's right." He tried to make his voice friendly. "You think maybe we ought to raise the bet?"

The kid did not hesitate. He said, "Five on the nine ball. Two on the five."

"Okay." Eddie said.

He let the kid score the nine twice in a row, just to salt the bet well, losing the last game by acting as if he were now, finally, playing his serious game of pool. He did this by cautiously running the balls from the one to the seven, then acting nervous and missing on the eight, making certain that he left a simple shot. This was a routine way of building confidence in the other man—to struggle through the difficult preliminaries and then choke up, letting him pick up an easy victory. It pleased Eddie to see the kid throw off his amateur game completely and try for style when he pocketed the eight and the nine.

"Say, kid," Eddie said, "you're one of the best."

The other player said nothing for a moment, just stood there with the sneer, one hand in his hip pocket, the other lightly holding his cue stick, his little finger sticking out delicately. Then he said, "You quitting, friend?"

Eddie stared at him. When he spoke he was astonished by the anger in his own voice. He did not grin. "No, kid," he said, levelly, "I'm not quitting." And then, "Suppose we play a game of hundred-dollar freeze-out. Ten games for ten a game, winner take all. Then we'll see who quits."

The kid looked at him coolly. *That's right,* Eddie thought, *you've got me now, boy. You smug little bastard.*

"Okay, friend," the kid said, "you're on."

They tossed, and Eddie won the break. And then, while the houseman was racking the balls, Eddie thought, *When I win this he'll quit anyway,* and he set his cue stick against the wall and began rolling up his sleeves, carefully, looking around him at the cheap, filthy place he was in, and then at the little easy table. He picked up his cue, chalked it. "Okay, punk," he said softly, "here we go."

He stepped up to the table, slipped easily into the old, automatic, easy form, stroked smoothly and powerfully, and slugged the nine ball in on the break, firing it into the corner pocket on a one-to-three shot. "That's one," he said, trying to grin, but his voice sounding strangely hard, grating, even to himself. And the sound of his voice shook him. You weren't supposed to feel this way, not on the hustle. And it was not wise—it was never wise—to look too good, not in a place like this one. He glanced at the group that was watching. Their faces seemed to have no expressions. *I'd better remember to lose a couple.*

It would be wiser not to try to make the nine on the break any more; the shot was too unreliable and showy. Instead, he would play this time for a wide spread and a second shot. He got it, slamming two balls in on the break; and then he ran the other seven off the table without pausing between shots or taking his eyes from the table. "That's two," he said. There was a little murmur in the group of men who were standing against the wall.

While the balls were being racked, he glanced at the kid, who was leaning against the next table now, a cigarette hanging from his mouth.

He won the next game by making an easy combination of the nine on his second shot. He ran out the balls, one through nine, in the fourth game. And when he did that something told him that he should not have, that he should not have looked that good. He would miss a ball the next game.

And then, when he was beginning to break, as the winner

always does in nine ball, as he was drawing back his cue, he heard the insolent voice, almost drawling, "You better not miss, friend," and he stopped his stroke, stared up at the kid and, then, laughed, coldly.

"I don't rattle," he said. "And, just for trying, I think I'll beat your ass flat."

It was simple. It was astonishingly simple. And fast. With the drop pockets and the little table and the quiet fury that he felt even in his cue stick he ran the next six games without even coming close to missing, making every shot perfectly. He slugged them in and eased them in and knifed them in, with dead-ball position.

When it was over the kid's sneer was gone and there was a buzzing—a fine, exalted buzzing—in Eddie's ears. When the kid threw the wadded-up bills out on the table, Eddie glanced at them, not picking them up, and said, "Are you quitting now, friend?"

The kid turned away from him and racked his cue. "Hell, yes, I'm quitting," trying, feebly, to shrug it off. Then he walked out of the poolroom, and Eddie suddenly remembered a time only a few weeks before when he had walked out of a poolroom himself, beaten and staggering and sick in his bowels; and he knew why he had despised, had hated, the snot-nosed, cheap, hustling kid who had seemed to be the same age as himself.

And then he looked up from the table to the five men who had been watching and knew, instantly, that he had made a mistake.

He was standing so that the table was behind him and the row of men in front. All of them had, it seemed, moved closer to him, and one of them, the one nearest the door, had shifted his position so that it would have been impossible to pass by him. They were all watching him closely. In the direct light from the two vibrating, bare bulbs their eyes seemed to flicker over him.

For a long while no one spoke. They seemed to be holding a position in a tableau. Then, not knowing what to do, Eddie broke it, pulling a cigarette from his pocket and putting it in his mouth—a weak gesture, but the only one he knew to make. Somewhere he was saying, wordlessly, *You goddamn fool,* saying it to himself. But that, too, was weak and meaningless. Something was about to happen, and only that had any meaning. He could hear the fan turning, shuddering its blades at each revolution, trembling the light bulbs on their black strings.

Then one of the men, an old man with pale eyes, said, his voice gurgling and obscene, "You're a pool shark, ain't you, boy? A real pool shark?"

Eddie said nothing. He let his eyes move to where the thick man, Turtle, was standing, his heavy lips in a pouting expression, his piglike eyes now malicious, staring at him contemptuously, and past him at the table. Then Turtle said, softly, "There's your money," nodding his head toward the table.

For a moment Eddie hesitated, wondering if this, the open, malicious contempt, was the only thing those piggish eyes were considering. He hesitated, and Turtle said again, "There's your money, boy," and then Eddie turned and reached out for the bills and before he had them in his hand—so quickly that he could not see it happen—the hot, stubby fingers were clamped around his wrist and the broad, ugly face was in his and the sentence that the man had only started was being finished with, ". . . you pool shark son of a bitch"—a private utterance, said deep in the throat and coming out into his face with the smell of hot, avid breath and the thick emphasis of hate.

He did not have time to be frightened before someone had taken the other arm and was pulling him, and Turtle was saying, now in a public voice, "Wait a minute. Let's give the son of a bitch his money." And then Turtle was, incongruously, tucking the bills into his, Eddie's, shirt pocket and saying, "We pay what we lose around here, boy," and peering at him from what seemed to have become a panorama of faces which he, Turtle, dominated in ugliness and in power. "But we don't like pool sharks," saying this now privately, confidentially, his face close, tucking the bills into the shirt pocket, tamping them down with his fingers, as if afraid they would be lost, as if Eddie might somehow ejaculate them from his pocket back on the table. "We got no use at all for pool sharks." Softly, wanting to make it perfectly clear.

Then they dragged him to the wooden toilet at the back of the room and two other men held him while Turtle carefully broke his thumbs. First the left one and then the right, taking them firmly on either side of the knuckle and bending them backward until the small bones in them broke.

Along the middle of the wall behind Eddie there was a two-by-four, to which the wall boards were nailed. On this was a row of empty bottles, and several of these fell to the floor from the jarring, jerking movements of Eddie's body, pinned against the wall. When the bottles hit they tinkled and jangled noisily; but Eddie did not hear them because of the overriding—yet distant, detached, far-off—sound of his own screaming.

13

HE WAS SITTING ON A STEP, his arms hanging at his sides. The step was cold, damp, and he was staring at it, at the dark triangle of concrete between his legs. Actually, he could not see it very well, for the light from the lamp at the street corner was weak. But this did not make any difference. Somebody had hit him in the side of the face, very hard, and now he was sick. The side of his face was sore, but his hands did not seem to feel anything, no pain at all, nothing.

Abruptly, he heard himself speak aloud. What he said was, *Anyway, it wasn't my wrists.* He was astonished, for he seemed to have been crying. He remembered now; but he did not lift his hands to look at them. He continued sitting on the step, in front of the door of Arthur's poolroom. He had beat on the door with his elbows and knees, his shoulders; he remembered all that. And some men had come out, suddenly, and hit him. . . .

After a while he heard someone coming down the street, but he did not look up. And then, in a moment, there was a voice, deep and resonant. "You go home now, boy. They closed."

He looked up. The man was a young Negro, perspiring and dressed gorgeously in a blue suit, looking at him strangely. He did not say anything and the Negro said, "Boy, you hurt. You go to the doctor." The man seemed to be swaying gently, and there was a worried look on his dark, shiny face. "Here, maybe you ought to have a drink." There was something ridiculously like a businessman about the way he pulled a pint bottle from his breast pocket. He opened it and held the bottle while Eddie took a long pull. Eddie wiped his mouth with his sleeve, careful not to look at his hand as he did this.

"Look, mister," the other man was saying, softly. "You better let me get you to a doctor. You been in some rough company."

The drink made him feel better. He was uncertain how to stand up; he did not want to push himself up with his hands.

"Help me up, please," he said.

The Negro helped him up, silently. "I'm all right," Eddie said. "Thanks."

The man squinted at him but did not protest. "You go get a doctor. Hear?"

"Sure," Eddie said. He started walking.

It seemed to be a very long time before he found a taxi. After he got in he had to think for a minute before he told the driver where to take him. Then he gave Sarah's address. The driver was a young man, and not talkative.

It was a long drive, and when they came into the more brightly lighted part of the city they stopped for a few moments at an intersection. In the weak light that came from the street corner, Eddie lifted his hands to his lap and looked at them.

Oddly, the surprise of them was only slight. They were twisted grotesquely, and the thumbs were askew. Above the knuckle of his right thumb there was a broken piece of bone showing, white, tinged with dark brown along one edge. There were a few blots of brown blood on his shirt sleeve and there was blood, like dried and cracking glue, on his wrist.

But they seemed to be someone's else's hands, not his own. Or like so much ruined meat. And there was no pain in them. . . .

He thought at first that Sarah was going to cry out when she saw him. She was reading when he came in, wearing her glasses and frowning, probably very drunk; but when she saw him her eyes flew wide.

"My God," she said.

He sat down. And suddenly he felt a tenseness in his stomach; it was beginning to start in his hands. The pain. "Get me a drink," he said.

"Sure." She got up quickly, no sign of drunkenness in her movement, poured a tumbler half full of bourbon and brought it to him. He did not have to tell her to hold it for him. He drank half of it and told her that was enough.

"How . . . do you feel?" she said.

"I don't know."

Her eyes had the puzzled look, and she was studying his face strangely. "What happened to you?"

"A lot of things." He was beginning to feel light-headed now, and bodiless. And, somehow, he was calm, calmer than he ever remembered having been. Nothing was very real. "I got beat up." Even his own voice sounded as if it were imaginary. "They broke my thumbs."

There was an incredulous look on her small face, a twisted and hurt look, and abruptly he realized that she must know a great deal about this kind of thing. Her polio, and whatever wrenching of her leg it had produced, whatever strange ways it had twisted her.

"Come on," she said, "I'll get you to a hospital."

There was an emergency room where the lights were too bright. The doctor was very old and had hands like a woman's, soft and moist. An intern gave Eddie a shot in his arm before the doctor began to work. There was something indecently soft about the doctor and Eddie distrusted him, hated him when he began insistently feeling then pulling on the thumbs. But then the room started becoming smaller and dimmer and he passed out.

After that he was sitting in a chair by the wall, his body stiff and sticky, his arms numb, weightless. The back of his neck was itching. He looked down and saw two white plaster casts enclosing the sides of his hands.

Sarah and the doctor were talking and the doctor was saying, ". . . at least four weeks. Probably more," and Sarah was asking about exercising the hands and the doctor said something about X-raying first, to find out about the sutures. He did not understand it, nor did he want to; but he watched Sarah, looking up at the doctor with her steady, wry look, getting all the facts straight. Sarah in this environment of white tile walls and oak chairs and steel needles and glass and the smells of alcohol and ether—another one of those strange and midnight worlds.

Finally he stood up, shakily, and said, "Let's get out."

She took him by the arm, gently, leading him outside. . . .

He had to wear the casts for two weeks. They were infuriating things, hampering all the simple motions, making the feeding of himself a stupid and fumbling act, forcing him to play the woman in bed. And even more than that they were an emasculation, destroying his old sense of power and reserve, the sense that derived more than anything else from a ridiculous ability to manipulate a stick of polished wood on a table with colored balls. Perhaps that was what Turtle had wanted: to humble him, to make him atone for that one brilliant and savage performance in the nine-ball game, to make him pay what is always extracted from talent and skill when they become, as they sometimes must, infuriated and belligerent. It was not the man he had beaten who had taken revenge; it was the man who had presided over the game. . . .

For the first several days he did not leave the apartment. He kept quiet most of the time, and did a good deal of thinking. Sometimes Sarah would talk to him—although she talked more than he wanted her to talk—telling him about her family or about some of the things she read. He put up with it, because there was nothing else to do.

She wrote a great deal. She would sit in the kitchen at the table, with her glasses on, for hours, over a portable typewriter, while he sat in the living room drinking or reading. Once, she attempted to read some of what she had written to him, but it made no sense. She explained that it was part of her thesis, something about a man named Keynes.

He was restless and he chafed at the inactivity, but he did not become morbid or really uncomfortable. Once, she rented a car and took him for a long ride and, finally, to a picnic, which she called a "surprise." He was, properly, surprised. She had brought sandwiches and a Thermos of gin and grapefruit juice. They both got drunk on the gin, in the quick, weird, and unsatisfactory way that you get drunk in sunlight, and the afternoon was merely awkward. They wound it up by quarreling over the slow way that she drove the car back home.

After a week he began going out. He went to a few poolrooms, vaguely looking for Bert, but he did not see him. Then he started going to movies in the afternoons, and that, although it passed time, was unpleasant, giving him headaches. He picked up a whore one afternoon and bought her some drinks, but was not interested when she proposed getting a room. She probably would have been enjoyable enough—she was young and had blatantly obscene breasts—but she wanted more money than he could afford. Also, he possibly owed Sarah something, he was not certain what.

And then Sarah took him to the doctor and the doctor took the casts off. His hands came out of their cocoons pale, white, and stiff. Moving them was very painful, and he dared not try to flex his thumbs. The doctor had told him not to try putting any pressure on them for a week or more.

That night they got drunker than usual, to celebrate, and he tried, carefully and persistently, to form a pool bridge—

the circle of curved forefinger and thumb that guides the thin end of the cue shaft—but it was impossible. This enraged him for a time. Sarah said nothing, but watched curiously as he attempted the manipulation. Then, when he grimaced once at a sudden stab of pain, she said, "You'd better leave it alone for a while. It hurts too much."

"How do you know how much it hurts?" he said, and then immediately realized that she had an answer for that one.

But she did not use the answer. What she said was, "It shows on you."

After a few days he found that he was able, after a fashion, to hold and swing the cue, at least on Sarah's kitchen table. He had to use the open-hand bridge—with the palm flat on the table, the thumb slightly raised, and the cue's end sliding in the groove between thumb and forefinger—and he held the big end of the stick just behind the balance with only the cupped fingers of his right hand, his thumb not supporting any weight. It was awkward, but he felt that he would be able to accomplish something that way.

One morning he was doing this, practicing on the table, trying to build up some kind of wrist action, to get flexibility into his stroke, which was still very painful. He had been doing this for more than an hour when Sarah came in, carrying a book, her thumb marking the place where she had stopped reading.

She sat and watched him silently for several minutes, and he paid no attention to her. Finally she said, "You look as if you know what you're doing with that . . . stick."

"I do," he said.

She watched him for another few minutes, and then she said, "How long have you been playing pool, Eddie?"

Her tone of voice was light enough; but he did not like it.

"Since I was about fourteen."

"Were you always good?"

"I started winning money when I was fifteen. Two—three dollars a day. Sometimes more." He grinned. "Sometimes I lost too."

"But not often."

"No." He swung the stick smoothly at an imaginary cue ball. "Not often . . ."

At Wilson's he practiced for three hours before the pain in his hands made him stop. He was crude and awkward, and even his stroke, the pendulum-like motion of his right arm, had suffered; but he could make balls. He kept lining them up and shooting them in, one after another.

He did not go back to Sarah's, but to a restaurant and then to a movie. The movie had to do with a deep-sea diver, and he watched it distractedly, not able to keep himself in spite of the pain from flexing his fingers, cautiously, carefully working his thumbs around, back and forth.

After the show he walked, through tired old residential avenues, along a honky-tonk street of bars, tattoo parlors and a penny arcade, and through streets where there seemed to be nothing but stores where women could buy clothes. He thought about buying something for Sarah, a silk nightgown or something, but then thought better of it. He had barely forty dollars—and nobody had said anything yet about the doctor bills.

When he got back to Sarah's she had already finished dinner: her dishes were piled, dirty, in the sink. She was in the living room, writing, the typewriter on her lap, when he came in.

He went into the kitchen, washed out a frying pan, and fried himself a frozen steak. He put this on a coffee saucer—one of the few remaining clean dishes in the cabinet—poured himself a glass of milk, got two slices of bread, stale, from the box on top of the stove, came into the living room, and sat beside Sarah on the couch. He made a sandwich with the bread and meat and began eating.

When he finished he looked at Sarah, grinned, and said, "Women, they tell me, are supposed to be real good at washing dishes."

She didn't look at him. "Is that right?" she said.

"That's right. And cooking too." He set the saucer down, reached over and patted her on the butt.

"Well, not this woman," she said. "And I wish you'd quit patting my rear. It doesn't thrill me in the least."

"It's supposed to," he said. "Maybe you're just different." And then, "You're funny, Sarah. Are all the women in Chicago like you?"

"How should I know? I don't know all the women in Chicago." She finished pecking a line out on the typewriter, and then looked at him, peering up over her glasses, her arms crossed over the typewriter in her lap. "I'm probably different, I suppose," she said, "'a horrible example of free thought.'"

"That sounds bad."

"It is. Fix me a drink."

He got up and poured her a glass of Scotch and water. He did not make one for himself. Then, when he gave it to her, he said, "I'll see you around," and headed for the door.

"Hey!" she said, and he turned. She was still looking up at him over her glasses. Her skin, in the light, seemed very white, transparent. Her blouse was thin, and beneath it he could see the outline of her small bosom, moving gently as she breathed.

"What is it?" he said.

She took a sip of her drink. "You've been out all afternoon."

Immediately he felt a thin edge of irritation in his voice. "That's right."

"So why go out now?"

He hesitated a moment, and then said, "So why not?"

She looked at him thoughtfully, a little coldly—there was a hardness that could come into her eyes—and then she said, softly, "No reason at all. Good night." She went back to the paper she was typing.

"Don't wait up for me," he said, going out the door. . . .

It was getting late when he walked into Wilson's, and there were only a few men there. On the back table was a very tall, elderly man, a straight-backed, white-haired man with a double-breasted gray suit. He was practicing and Eddie, standing at the counter in the front of the room, watched him for several minutes. The man shot stiffly—he looked to be at least sixty years old—but he was good. He was practicing at straights, and he knew the game; Eddie could tell from the way he controlled the cue ball, making it lie down when he wanted it to without any wild English or long, haphazard rolls. He did not seem to have the stroke of a real first-rate player, for he lacked the smoothness and the gentle, precise wrist action; normally he would have been considerably below Eddie's league.

Eddie asked the withered man behind the counter for a package of cigarettes, and when he got them asked quietly who the man on the back table was.

The old man grinned like a conspirator and wheezed, in the obscene voice that some old men have, "That man's a real pool hustler," he said. "That's Bill Davis from Des Moines. Probably just come from up at Bennington's. He's one of the real big boys."

Eddie had heard of him somewhere; he was supposed to be, as well as he could remember, a small-time hustler.

"What's his game?" he asked.

"How's that?"

"What's his best game? What does he play?"

"Oh." The man behind the counter bent closer to him. "Straights," he said. "Straight pool."

That's nice, Eddie thought, walking back toward where the man was practicing. But then you had to be steady to play good straights. He was not certain that he could trust his hands that much yet. Maybe it would be smarter to try getting him into a game of one-pocket. In one-pocket you depend more on brainwork and on patience—qualities that you don't have to rely on your hands for. And every straight pool hustler plays one-pocket; the old man was sure to know the game. And, then, that made Eddie wonder, suddenly, if the tall man would know him, Fast Eddie Felson, by reputation, or had seen him play somewhere else. The thought of it, of losing his first chance for a good, workable game in weeks, made him suddenly feel tight, even nervous. But in a moment he laughed at himself; he was thinking as Bert must think, analyzing, planning out the angles, figuring the odds. It amused him to think of little, tight, lip-pursing Bert, sitting on one of those stools back there, eating potato chips and telling him how he had everything figured out. But then, Bert did drive a new car. Every year.

He leaned against the near table and watched Bill Davis shoot out a rack of balls. When Davis finished he racked up the fourteen of them into the triangle and attempted a straight-pool break shot off the fifteenth, banking the colored ball into the side of the triangle and trying to make it skid off into the near corner. The ball hit the rail a few inches short of the pocket. Davis worked with great intensity at the shot, bending over the cue ball grimly, and then swooping down on it like a hawk. When he had missed he let out his breath in a great gasp, and began wiping his forehead.

Eddie tried to look sympathetic. "That sure was a tough one," he said.

The man turned around, facing him, looked at him a moment, and then grinned. His teeth were huge, white and even. Eddie wondered if they were false. "You sure right," the man said. His voice practically boomed, and he spoke with a thick accent. "That shot is sure one tough shot of pool." His voice was loud and he spoke with what sounded like great conviction, earnestness.

Eddie smiled at him. "You can't make 'em all."

"That's right. You sure can't make 'em all." The voice and the grin were both enormous, and Eddie was a little dumbfounded by them. "I only wish you could. I been playing this goddamn game fifteen years and I sure don't know one man yet make all those goddamn balls, I sure don't." The man's voice was softer now, and Eddie was relieved, although he still was not certain what to make of him. It struck him that perhaps Davis should be a con man of some kind; he seemed to be one of the most trustworthy types Eddie had ever seen—his voice vibrated with honesty and seriousness.

Eddie watched him rack the balls and then he said, "You like to play a game or two?"

"Sure, I like to play. What game?" He slammed the rack on the table and began piling the balls fiercely into it. His hands were huge, strong-looking, and rough, and he handled the balls as if they were golf balls.

"Is one-pocket all right?"

"Fine." The man fished vigorously in his pocket and withdrew a half dollar. He threw this in the air, over the table. "Which side comes up?" he said.

"Tails."

It came up heads; Davis would break. In one-pocket, unlike straight pool, the break is an advantage; with it you can nudge a good many balls over to the side of the table where your scoring pocket is, and if you know how to do it right you can invariably leave the other man perfectly safe—without a possible shot.

The man began chalking his cue and said, "You want to play for some money? A few dollars?"

Eddie grinned. "Ten?"

The old man raised his eyebrows, which were gray and very shaggy. *"Fine."*

When he got up to the head of the table to break the balls

he bent down stiffly, pumped his cue stick vigorously several times, stopped, aimed, pumped again, and then shot. His concentration was so great that a large soft vein, purplish, stood out on his forehead. The break was very good, although not perfect.

Eddie decided that, from the start, there would be no point in playing down his own game. He was not certain, anyway, that he would be able to win even by playing his best. There would be no point in throwing off, underplaying himself, just to set up a big game or two that he might lose.

So he played carefully, using his open-hand bridge and his awkward hold on the cue, and shot the best that he could. Any ten-dollar bills that he could pick up he could use. He played cautiously, making most of his shots defensive, trying for a ball only when he was certain he could make it, and he beat the man by a close score—eight to six.

They played another and Eddie won that. The man was good, but wild—and not smart enough. He lost the third, but won the one afterward. When they had finished that game, Davis grinned at him and said, "How come you shoot flat hand? You sure too goddamn good to shoot like that all the time."

"I hurt my hands. In an accident."

They kept on playing and after a few hours Eddie had won ninety dollars. But his hands were beginning to ache, and he began to shoot stiffly, afraid that he would put pressure on one of his thumbs and the pain would stab through it. The old man's vigor did not abate: he was one of the professionals like Minnesota Fats—although not nearly as good—in his tireless, consistently good game. And he was funny. Once, in the middle of a game, Davis was bending rigidly over the cue ball at the end of the table, concentrating, his forehead vein purplish, on a difficult shot, when suddenly he drew back and stood erect, his great hands on his hips, staring toward the center of the table. Eddie looked and saw a small black insect walking unconcernedly across the green, in the line of the old man's shot. The thing was the size of a gnat, with no wings.

Davis was staring at it, his eyes bulging apoplectically. Finally, the bug stopped, turned around, and began walking back the way it had come.

Davis glared. "You little black son of a bitch," he said, "you had your goddamn chance, you sure had." Then, suddenly, he swooped forward, and with the small end of his cue stick extended, delivered a very rapid series of short taps, as if trying to hammer the bug through the table. Then he bent forward and, with deliberation, flicked the corpse off the table, using a massive thumb and forefinger. "That's teach you *good,* you son of a bitch," he said.

And playing him, Eddie slowly became aware of something he had not been aware of about himself for a long time: of how much he enjoyed playing pool. Things of that kind, things that simple, can be forgotten easily—especially in all of the questions of money and gambling, talent and character, born winner and born loser—and they can come as a shock. Eddie loved to play pool. There was a kind of power, a kind of brilliant coordination of mind and of skill, that could give him as much pleasure, as much delight in himself and in the things that he did, as anything else in the world. Some men never feel this way about anything; but Eddie had felt it, as long as he could remember, about pool. He loved the hard sounds the balls made, loved the feel of the green wool cloth under his hand, the other hand gently holding the butt of his cue, tapping leather on ivory.

And then, after he had won three games in a row, the big man grinned broadly, toothily, at him and said, "I quit you now. You too goddamn good."

"Sure," Eddie said, grinning. He took the final ten from him and, putting it in his billfold, hardly noticed the tugging of acute pain in his hands. Everything, it seemed, about this game had been perfect: they had even quit at the right time. He was not certain; but he figured that he had won at least a hundred and a half. He could use it.

"You want a drink?" he said to the other man, affably. They had drunk nothing but coffee during the playing.

"*Sure.*" His voice boomed out again, like it had done at first, "You buy me a martini?"

"Be glad to," Eddie said.

They went to the back room and washed their hands, getting the grime and chalk off them. The big man washed as he did everything else, like a zealot. "What's your name, anyway?" he said. "You shoot so goddamn good I should know your name. For next time."

Eddie laughed. "Felson," he said. "Eddie Felson."

"Eddie Felson?" The big man thought about this for a moment. "*Sure.*" In the little washroom, his voice could have broken mirrors, cracked porcelain. "Somebody told me about you. Fast Eddie, is that it?"

"That's it."

"*Say.*" He held out a huge hand. "My name's Bill Davis. From Des Moines, Iowa."

Eddie took the hand apprehensively, afraid the man would

squeeze it. But he shook gently, aware, apparently, of the soreness. "You're one damn finc pool player. When you get your hands fixed up you must be one of the best."

"Thanks," Eddie said.

"Maybe I should buy *you* a drink."

"That's okay, I can afford it," Eddie said, grinning.

The martini glass seemed lost in Davis' hand. He gulped it and then set the glass down on the counter. For a moment Eddie was afraid he would slam it down as he had the pool triangle, slivering glass everywhere. "You know," he said, "if I had the chance to learn how to shoot pool when I was a boy I would be one damn fine good pool player myself."

"You shoot good right now," Eddie said.

"Sure. Sure, I shoot good. I beat most people I play. But I'm an old man. I was an old man first time in my life I saw a pool table. Fifteen years ago. First year I come to the States to live."

"You mean there aren't any pool tables where you come from?"

"I don't know. Maybe some. But in Albania—I come from Albania fifteen goddamn years ago—I'm always a working man. Mechanic. I save my money and come here to buy a business. I buy a garage. No goddamn good—nobody makes money in a garage. So I buy a poolroom, cheap, in Des Moines, Iowa. Now I'm sixty-eight years old and I'm just learning to play this goddamn game of pool." Then he grinned, his big, horsy teeth flashing, "But I like it. It's the best goddamn game there is."

It seemed impossible that the man could be sixty-eight. He should be tired, if he were, or vague. But the deep lines in his face, like ruts, and the thousands of tiny, fine lines between the heavy ones were the kind that took years to grow. The man was impossible, some kind of natural phenomenon.

Abruptly he got up, slapped Eddie on the back, said, "You sure a goddamn pool player, Eddie Felson." Then he walked out the door, taking big strides, his back stiff, erect, his arms swinging, stiffly, at his sides. . . .

By the time Eddie got home he felt great. He had stopped in a drugstore to pick up a box of candy for Sarah, and when he got there he woke her up and handed the box to her.

"What in hell is that?" she said, her voice thick with sleep and liquor.

"Candy," he said. "Whole damn box full of it. For you."

She was sitting up, slumped, in bed, her hair falling over her forehead and her eyes gluey. She blinked, "What in hell's the idea?"

"A present. A gift."

She tossed it loosely down to the foot of the bed, and then fell over on her side, away from him. "Just what I need," she said. And then, "Where have you been? Shooting pool?" He could not tell if it were sleepiness or bitterness in her voice, but the tone of it was dead.

"That's right."

Abruptly, she rolled over and looked at him, balefully. "Eddie . . ." and then she rolled back. "Never mind. You wouldn't know what I was talking about."

His voice had become very cold. "I probably wouldn't," he said.

14

FOR SEVERAL DAYS HE PRACTICED, working at it doggedly each time until the pain in his hands became too great for him to continue. It did not make him feel good to do it, but there was a kind of cathartic effect. And it was like the old days in Oakland—those years when he had practiced daily with concentration and intensity, back when to become a great pool hustler was, for him, the finest and the best thing for him to want of his life. He did not have as much of the certainty or the conviction, now—although to think of himself as an insurance salesman or a shoe clerk would have only been absurd—but the game, and the hard, absorbing, almost religious practicing were a reminder to him of what he was, of what he had been and was going to be. And it kept him from thinking, kept him from being irritated with all of the vague issues that had been pestering him since the day he had walked into Bennington's, and even before.

One afternoon he was shooting on the back table at Wilson's, lining the balls down the middle of the table and knifing them into the side pockets, when Bert came in.

Bert was wearing a conservative—or cautious—brown business suit. When he saw Eddie his thin lips pressed into a slight, thin smile. "Hello," he said.

Eddie slammed a ball he had been aiming at into the side pocket. Then he leaned gently on his cue and said, "Hi. Where've you been?"

Bert took a seat, adjusting his trouser legs as he sat down. "Here and there," he said, with no particular tone of voice.

"How's business?"

He pursed his lips. "Business is slow."

There was nothing else to say just then. Eddie began shooting the balls again, conscious that Bert was watching him and, in all probability, judging him.

When he had finished out the rack, Bert spoke, "Why the open-hand bridge? Is there something wrong with the hands?"

Eddie grinned at him. "An accident. At Arthur's."

He expected Bert to say something to the effect of "I told you so," but Bert did not. He said, "Oh?" and raised his pale eyebrows. "You seem to do all right that way."

"Fair." Eddie began racking the balls. "I'd say my game was maybe twenty per cent off. Maybe more."

"If that's right you aren't in too bad a shape. What happened? They step on your hands?"

"Thumbs," Eddie said, shooting. "A big bastard broke them."

Bert seemed interested. "Man named Turtle Baker?"

Eddie couldn't help looking surprised. "You know everybody, don't you?"

Bert seemed very pleased with this. "Everybody who can hurt me," he said, pursing his lips again, "and everybody who can help me. It pays."

Eddie began working on corner pocket shots, the thin cuts where the cue ball must be given a natural roll. Finally he said, "You should give me lessons."

Bert looked at him thoughtfully. "Sign up."

Eddie did not answer but went back to the shooting, flicking the colored balls on the side with the white ball, making them edge gently into the pocket, while the cue ball went hurtling around the table. The shot was a pleasant one to shoot; possibly it was the combination of sped and slowness, and the inevitability of the motions when it was shot right. Then, finally, when he had finished with the fifteen balls, he looked up at Bert again. "Where do I sign?"

Bert adjusted his steel-rimmed glasses on his nose. "For Lexington?"

"For anywhere you say." Eddie grinned. "Boss."

Bert's eyes were wide, seeming even wider under the thick glasses. "What happened to you?"

"Like I said. My thumbs."

"I don't mean the thumbs. You already told me about the thumbs."

Eddie thought about this a minute. Then he said, "Maybe I've been thinking."

"Thinking about what?"

"About how maybe I'm not such a high-class piece of property right now. And about how maybe playing for a twenty-five per cent slice of something big is better than playing for nickles and dimes."

"Well," Bert said, leaning back in his chair, his small hands folded delicately on his lap. "Of course, with your hands in the condition they're in . . ."

Eddie grinned. "You can come off that right now. You know damn well I can beat your Findlay, thumbs or no thumbs. And they didn't break my 'character' at Arthur's. That's what you said was wrong with me, remember?"

"I remember," Bert said. He paused a few minutes, apparently in deep concentration, his little pink hands with the impeccable fingernails twitching mildly in his soft lap. Finally he said, "All right. Day after tomorrow. Seven o'clock in the morning."

Eddie blinked at him. "Seven in the morning? What in hell for? I haven't been up at that time of night since I was going to Sunday school."

Bert smiled. "You should never of quit going to Sunday school. You're the type. You look like you've got morals."

"Thanks. You look like Santa Claus."

"Oh, I've got morals too. I was brought up right. Only you look like you've got the good kind of morals. Anyway, you get up and meet me just like going to Sunday school, day after tomorrow, right here at seven o'clock. That way we can drive to Lexington in a day." And then, his voice more easy, "I don't like to get up at seven either."

"Okay," Eddie said, "I'll bring my cue."

"And one more thing," Bert said. "I'm paying all the expenses and I'm taking all the risks. So while you're with me you'll play it my way."

"I figured to," Eddie said, not looking up at him. He bent down, concentrating on a long shot on the four ball, which sat, a quiet sphere of dull purple, in the middle of the table. He took careful aim, swung powerfully, and hammered it into the far corner pocket. The cue ball came to a dead stop. He looked over at Bert.

Bert was climbing down slowly from the high chair, his smooth, babyish face with a pleased expression, the look of a man well content with his small and comfortable world. "Come on," he said to Eddie.

"Where?"

"I'm buying you a drink. Now that we're in business together . . ."

15

HE PRACTICED FOR MOST OF THE NEXT DAY, and when he was finished was afraid that he had overdone it; his thumbs seemed to be even stiffer and more sore. But there would be time for them to loosen up, tomorrow, during the trip.

He was not certain how to tell Sarah that he was leaving—he had not even told her about the money he'd won from Bill Davis—and he did not know exactly what to expect from her. Obviously, the best thing was to be diplomatic about it: get her properly drunk and then bring it up.

It was four in the afternoon when he finished practicing, and he went immediately from the poolroom to Sarah's. She was working on her writing, in the kitchen, when he came in. He walked into the room, turned the fire on under the remains of the breakfast coffee, sat down at the table opposite her and said, "What kind of outfit can you buy for fifty dollars?"

She peered over at him, looking over her glasses, the old

puzzled expression on her face. She was wearing a white shirt with the tail out, and a green corduroy skirt. "You mean dress, shoes, hat?"

"That's right."

"A fair one. It's summer; summer clothes are cheaper. Why?"

He pulled a cigarette out and lit it. "Seventy-five dollars?"

"A good outfit. Damn good. What's it for? And who?"

"For you. For dinner. Tonight."

She took her glasses off, frowning. "I don't need clothes. And what's happening tonight?"

"What's happening tonight is we're going out for dinner. At the best place you can pick." He got up, cut the fire off under the coffee and began searching for a clean cup. "And you can use some clothes."

"Now wait a minute. What's the plan, Eddie? First it's candy—at two o'clock in the morning. Now clothes. Where did you get the money?"

He found and began rinsing out a cup. "A man gave it to me."

"Sure." She looked away from him. "Playing pool?"

"That's right."

"Great. That's fine. Where do I fit in on this? Why give me a cut? Is your conscience bad?"

"Look," he said, "maybe I should forget it."

"Maybe you should. You don't have to buy me things. You've already seduced me, remember?"

He drank off half the cup of coffee. It was lukewarm and foul. "I remember." He set the cup, unfinished, back in the sink. "Do you want the clothes? Somebody told me, once, that women like clothes. And candy."

Her voice was hard. "Your logic's overwhelming. Who told you *I* like clothes and candy? And going out to dinner?"

"Nobody. Forget it." He went into the living room, sat down and picked up a news magazine. Somebody was fighting a war and he read about this, although it was not interesting. Her typewriter kept banging for several minutes and then stopped. Then he heard her clinking ice and glasses. In a minute she came in and held out a highball.

She smiled slightly. "Sometimes," she said, "I'm a bitch."

"That's right." He took the drink.

She sat on the footstool that was in front of his chair, and began working on her drink silently. He set his magazine down and looked at her. The shirt she was wearing was like a man's shirt, and the top two buttons were undone. Her brassiere was loose and looking down he could see her nipples. This amused him at first, for the hustle in it was obvious. He knew very well that there is nothing accidental that women do with their bosoms.

Finally she looked up at him again, grinning a little wryly, self-consciously. "Do you still want to take me out?" The breath that she took, after saying this, was just a bit exaggerated, heaving the breasts up.

He could not help laughing. "Okay," he said, reaching down and taking her under the arms. "You win. We'll buy the dress, afterward."

"We'd better hurry," she said. "The stores'll be closing." He took her by the arm, leading her into the bedroom.

Afterward he lay on his back in bed, perspiring. He felt very good, very relaxed. And there was a good feeling in his stomach, the feeling of something about to begin. There would be new places to go, new games to play. Sarah was smoking a cigarette in bed, looking thoughtful and at ease, her small body covered with the sheet.

She rolled over and stubbed her cigarette out, leaning across him in bed so that her hair fell down over her face as she mashed the cigarette in the ash tray. Then she looked down at him and grinned. "Let's go," she said. . . .

She tried to act as if buying the clothes meant nothing to her, but he could see that she was enjoying it. She would act cynical about every outfit she looked at, but he noticed that she was very careful about what she bought. And what she finally did buy looked tremendous on her: a navy blue dress, tight and perfectly fitting, that made her butt gorgeous, navy blue shoes, unornamented, a navy blue and white hat, and white gloves.

She was in the bathroom for what seemed like an hour. It took him twenty minutes to put on a clean shirt and socks and to shave, and he spent the rest of the time reading about the war and about a lot of people who were supposed to be interesting because they were rich or actors or both.

"Hey!" he said, getting up and walking to her. And she smelled good; he had never known her to use perfume before. "You're the best. The best there is."

He could almost feel her effort to keep her voice wry, "Thanks." She looked at him and said, "And if you want to do this right you'd better change that suit. It's wrinkled."

He laughed. "Sure."

He had one dress shirt and a tie and he put these on together with his gray suit. When he came out she laughed. "I never saw you with a tie before. You look like a fraternity president."

"And you're the sweetheart of whatever it is. Let's go."

As they were going out the door she stopped him for a moment, looked up at him and said, "Eddie. Thanks."

She picked the place they went to. She had heard of it, but never been there. It was precisely the kind of restaurant he had in mind—big, dimly lit, quiet, elegantly furnished. He liked it immediately and, deciding to play it out all the way, gave the headwaiter a five and picked out his own table, by a wall. The five earned them a bowing and impeccable waiter and Sarah started them off with a bottle of cocktail sherry that was as old as she was. One odd thing: he was surprised that Sarah was imposed on by the place, a little nervous, defensive, and awkward; whereas he felt thoroughly at home himself, even though he had hardly ever been in this kind of restaurant in his life. But after two glasses of the wine and after the band began playing quiet, light music, she began to loosen up. He was beginning to feel very fine and he began talking to her about himself—a thing that he seldom did. But he did not tell her about Minnesota Fats. And then when they were through eating and were drinking the tiny glasses of Benedictine which she had ordered and which he found he did not like, he leaned forward, his elbows on the table, and said, "I suppose you know I had a reason."

A moment before her face had been alive. Immediately it became hard. "There's always an angle, isn't there?"

"I don't play the angles. Not with you."

"Sure." There was no conviction in her voice. She finished her glass of Benedictine, settled back in her seat and folded her arms across her chest. "All right, what is it, Eddie?"

He looked at her coolly, "I'm leaving town for a while."

Her eyes darted to his face and then, quickly, away. There was no expression in them, only a kind of curiosity. He knew, however, that this was a pose, and he knew as any gambler would know that there was a reason for it, in the game that they had begun to play—the game that he himself, in fact, had hustled her into a long time before. He did not, however, know what the pose was intended to conceal. With Sarah, he was never quite certain.

She looked back at him steadily. Then she said, "For how long, Eddie?" She might have been asking him if he wanted another cup of coffee.

"I don't know."

"A week? A year?"

"More like a week. I'll be back."

She began putting on her gloves. She did this as she did many things, deftly, yet with care. "Sure," she said. She stood up. "Let's go home."

Outside they walked silently. There were pockets in the skirt of her dress and by jamming her hands in these she was able, magically, to convert what had been a chic appearance a moment before into the kind of wistful, limping dowdiness that seemed to be her most natural pose in the outside world.

After several minutes he said, gently, "Don't you want to know where I'm going?"

"No. Yes, I want to know where you're going, and what for. Only I don't want to ask."

"I'm going to Kentucky," he said. "Lexington. With a friend."

She did not say anything, but kept walking, her hands in her pockets still, her eyes straight ahead.

"I'm going to try to make some money. I need it, the money." And suddenly he cursed himself, silently, for the apology that had been in his voice. He had nothing to apologize to her for. He made his voice carefully matter of fact, "I'm leaving early in the morning."

She looked at him for a moment. Her voice was like ice water, "Leave now."

He looked at her, with the quick irritation that she could make him feel. "Grow up," he said.

She didn't look at him again. "All right, maybe I should grow up. But why in hell didn't you tell me sooner? Is that the way pool sharks do? Here today, gone tomorrow, like the gamblers in the movies?"

He had never liked to hear anyone say "pool shark," and he did not like to hear her say it. "I didn't know sooner," he said.

"Sure you didn't. Big deal coming up in Lexington, I bet. All the big card sharps, confidence men. Maybe even Frank Costello, Lucky Luciano, is that it?"

He did not say anything for a while. They were nearing her place, and he took her inside and sat down before he spoke. "I'm going to Kentucky to play pool with a man named Findlay. I need the action and I need the money. And that's it. If you want to you can probably come with me."

Abruptly, she started laughing, standing in the middle of the big and shabby living room. "Just what I need," she said. The arrogance and self-pity in her pose embarrassed and angered him. He turned away from her, looking at the large picture of the clown on the wall, which he liked. She had stopped the laughing, but the sarcasm in her voice kept him from looking at her. "No, Eddie," she said. "I'll wait for you. Your faithful little piece of tail. How'll that be?"

This last, the phoniness of it, suddenly changed his anger to something else. He turned to look at her, standing, now, staring at him, her small hands jammed in her pockets, her feet wide apart. It occurred to him that she was like a small sick thing in a jar, a fluttering, shrill insect that he could have poked with a stick, could prod, when he wanted to.

"That would be fine," he said, his voice strange to him, but easy. "You make a very good piece of tail. One of the best."

She stared at him. "Eddie," she said, her voice trembling, "you're probably a cheap crook. It just occurred to me."

"The hell it just did." His voice was cool and level. "It's been occurring to you for a damn long time already. Probably excites the pee out of you, too—shacking up with a criminal."

"All right. Maybe it does. Or did. And maybe I'm beginning to learn what a criminal is."

He looked at her with open contempt. "You've got no goddamn idea what a criminal is. You got no goddamn idea what I am either. You wouldn't know a crook from a bartender. Who the hell do you think you are, calling me a crook? What do you know about what I do for a living?" He turned away from her again. "Get me a drink."

He did not hear her move or breathe for a long moment. Then she walked into the kitchen. He heard her fixing drinks.

When she came back in she did not look as though he had

beaten her—or even stalemated her—but he knew that her front was one of the best he had ever seen. He began to wonder, with some interest, what was going to happen next. He was beginning to enjoy himself.

Finally she said, "All right. You win again. You always win." And then, "Only, next time, let me know a little in advance, will you?"

"Sure. If I can."

What she said next she said as if she were talking to herself, ruminating, meditating aloud, "If there is a next time . . ."

He did not want to let that go by. He felt a little as Bert must feel, felt like pushing, getting it out, crowding her.

"Why not a next time?" he said.

But she did not answer that. Instead she looked at him, her eyes blazing again, suddenly, and said, "Do you know what you've gotten out of me—what I've given you?"

"What?"

"Among other things, myself."

Suddenly, he felt like laughing. "And you think you shouldn't have given that? You should have sold it, maybe."

She hesitated before she spoke. "How low can you hit, Eddie?" she said.

"Maybe you're trying to collect now, maybe that's it. Only you never gave me a thing, without taking, and you know it. I never hustled you—even when I thought I was hustling you—and you know that too. What you give me is below your waist, and that's all of it. And that's the only thing I give you. What else do you want, for what you're offering?"

She seemed to be desperate for a word that would cut him

down. She took the coward's way out. "Love," she said, as if the word were important in some abstract way.

He stared at her and then grinned. "That's something else you wouldn't know if you saw it walking down the street. And I wouldn't either."

She took a gulp of her drink. "What are you trying to do to me? I love you, for Christ's sake."

He looked at her steadily and she seemed even more like an insect trying to escape from a jar, a jar with slippery, transparent, glass walls. "That's a goddamn lie," he said.

For more than a minute she was silent, looking at him.

"All right, Eddie," she said. "You've won. Rack up your cue. You always win."

He stared at her. "That's more crap," he said. But he did not say it well; she had gotten through.

"The way you're looking at me," she said, her eyes wide, hurt and angry, but her voice level. "Is that the way you look at a man you've just beaten in a game of pool? As if you had just taken his money and now what you want is his pride?"

"All I want is the money."

"Sure," she said. "Sure. Just the money. And the aristocratic pleasure of seeing him fall apart." She looked at him more calmly now. "You're a Roman, Eddie," she said. "You have to win them all."

He turned his face away, toward the orange clown. He did not like what she was saying. "Nobody wins them all."

"No," she said. "No, I suppose not."

And suddenly he turned to her, seeing for the first time what seemed to be the whole truth of Sarah, in a moment's flash of wonder and contempt. "You're a born loser, Sarah," he said.

Her voice was soft. "That's right," she said. She remained seated on the couch, upright, holding her drink in both hands protectively, as if holding a child or a child's doll. Her elbows were on her knees, her lips tightly together, and she was no longer looking at him. It took him a moment to realize what she was doing. She was crying.

He said nothing, for there came to him a strange and ambivalent thing, twisting him, distorting his vision and yet making it so sharp that he felt that he could see anything—around corners, through walls, into the eye of the sun—there came into his mind, with a kind of pleasant contempt, the words that Bert had used with him: *self-pity. One of the best indoor sports.*

Then, suddenly, she looked back up to him and said, "And you're a winner, Eddie. A real winner . . ."

16

BERT WAS EXACTLY ON TIME, in the morning. It was a warm, fine, beautiful morning, a glistening, late-summer morning; but Eddie was hardly aware of this. He was awake; he had come sharply awake at four-thirty, to the sounds of shrill and infrequent birds and to a kind of cold turbulence within his own mind; but he hardly saw the thing that the morning had to show him—the city of Chicago, Illinois, in a state of grace. He leaned back in the large, well-upholstered seat of Bert's car, held his small leather case in his lap, and kept his mind from thinking, or feeling.

Bert drove as he played poker, sitting erect, his lips tight, his eyes fixed ahead, missing nothing. He, too, was silent. They hardly spoke until noon, although there was no tension between them. What went on in Bert's mind was unfathomable; Eddie would not have been certain what was going on in his own.

They stopped along the road for hamburgers and coffee, and Eddie had a quick drink, although Bert declined one. Afterward, in the car he looked at Bert and said, wanting now to talk, "What do they play in Kentucky, what's the big game?"

Bert, as always, thought for a moment before he spoke. "They play bank pool," he said, "and one-pocket."

"Good," Eddie said. "I like that about one-pocket. What does Findlay play?"

Bert paused again. "I don't know. I never saw him play. I only know him from his poker days."

Eddie grinned. "You must have a lot of confidence in me."

"I don't."

"Then how do you know he won't beat me? How do you know he won't shoot better pool than I do?"

"I don't know that. And I don't have much confidence in you. But I got confidence in Findlay."

"What does that mean?" Eddie withdrew a cigarette from his pocket and lit it.

"It means I got confidence that Findlay's a loser, all the way a loser. And you happen to be only about one-half loser, the other half winner."

"How do you figure that?"

Bert stretched himself behind the wheel and then allowed himself to relax slightly, although he continued to watch the road carefully as he spoke. "I told you," he said. "I already watched you lose—watched you lose to a man you should of beat."

Bert was beginning to take the old line again, and Eddie did not like it. "Look," he said. "I already told you . . ."

"I know what you already told me," Bert said. "And I don't

want to hear it again, not right now." And then, when Eddie did not reply to this, Bert took a breath and said, "What I'm thinking about is you and Findlay personally—not the game of pool you're going to play. Any way he shoots pool he probably shoots good enough to beat you if you want to let him and if he's got the character for it. But he hasn't, that's the point."

Bert drove silently for a few minutes, pushing the big car along at a steady sixty-five. Then he said, "Unless you're in a game with a sap or a drunk, when you're playing for the large money you play the man himself more than you ever play the game. Like in poker, in a really worthwhile poker game, everybody knows how to play the odds, everybody knows how it stands with filling straights and flushes, with figuring the pot and counting out the cards—I knew all that when I was fifteen. But the man who wins the games is the man who watches for the big money and pulls his guts together and gives himself character enough to stare down five other men and make the bet that nobody else would think of making and follow through with it. It's not luck—there's probably no such thing as luck, and if there is you can't depend on it. All you can do is play the percentages, play your best game, and when that critical bet comes—in every money game there is always a critical bet—you hold your stomach tight and you push hard. That's the clutch. And that's where your born loser loses."

Eddie thought about this a minute. Then he said, "Maybe you're right."

"But you got to know when the clutch in the game is," Bert said, his voice becoming more insistent now. "You got to know and you got to bear down, no matter what kind of voice is telling you to relax. Like when you were playing pool with Minnesota Fats, when you had him beat and you were so tired your eyeballs were hanging out, and when something was gonna have to give somewhere—either you or Fats." Bert stopped a minute, and when he spoke again his voice was hard, direct and certain. "You know when that was? When it was that Fats knew he was gonna beat you?"

"No."

"Okay, I'll tell you. It was when Fats went to the toilet and you flattened out in a chair. Fats knew the game was in the clutch, he knew he had to do something to stop it, and he played smart. He went back to the john, washed his face, cleaned his fingernails, made his mind a blank, combed his hair, and then came back ready. You saw him; you saw how he looked—clean again, ready to start all over, ready to hold tight and push hard. And you know what you were doing?"

"I was waiting to play pool."

"That's right," Bert said. "Sure. You were waiting to get your ass beat. You were flattened out on your butt, swimming around in glory and in whiskey. And, probably, you were deciding how you could lose."

For a moment Eddie did not answer, feeling an unreasoning anger, a kind of wild irritation. . . . Then he said, "What makes you know so goddamn much? What makes you know what I think about when I shoot pool?"

"I just know," Bert said. And then, "I been there myself, Eddie. We've all been there. . . ."

Eddie did not say anything, but sat, the irritation still tight in his stomach and the slight, irritating, itching pain in his hands.

He wanted to fight something, to hit out at something, but he did not know what. He watched the road ahead of them, and after a while he began to feel calmer.

And then, after more than an hour, Bert said, "That's what the whole goddamn thing is: you got to commit yourself to the life you picked. And you picked it—most people don't even do that. You're smart and you're young and you got, like I said before, talent. You want to live fast and loose and be a hero."

"Be a hero? Who the hell said what I want?"

"I did. You and any decent goddamn gambler wants to be a hero. But to be a hero you got to sign a contract with yourself. If you want the glory and the money you got to be hard. I don't mean you got to get rid of mercy, you're not a con man or a thief—those are the ones that can't live if they got mercy. I got it myself. I got soft places. But I'm hard with myself and I know when not to go weak. Like when you give the business to a woman; you got to give it; don't hold back. Do your second-guessing afterward. Or before. But with a woman you make a contract—I don't know what all the words are in the contract but it's there and if you don't know about it you're not human, I don't care what all the slobs and the bastards and the free love people say. And when you give it to the woman or when you make the contract that says, 'I'm gonna beat your ass in this game of pool,' you don't hold back. Don't let the little squirrel on your back that says, 'Keep free of it; don't give yourself away,' talk you into anything. Make the squirrel shut up. Don't try to kill him; you need him there. But when he starts telling you there wasn't any contract, make him shut up. And when you come to that certain time in the game he says, 'Don't stick your neck out. Be smart. Hold back,' not because he wants to save your money for you, but because he doesn't want to lose you, doesn't want to see you put your goddamn heart into the game. He wants you to lose, wants to see you being sorry for yourself, wants you to come to him for sympathy."

Eddie looked at him. "And if you lose?"

"Then you lose. When you're a winner, it hurts your soul to lose. But your soul can take being hurt."

Eddie was not certain of what it all meant. But after a while he said, "Maybe you're right."

"I know I'm right," Bert said.

They passed through Cincinnati late in the afternoon, a crowded, gray city, and crossed a bridge into Kentucky. After a while there were a great many fields of a tall, broad-leafed kind of plant and, passing one of these fields, Eddie said, "What is that stuff, cabbage?"

Bert laughed. "That's tobacco."

Eddie looked at the big plants for a moment, a huge field of them. "What do you know?" he said. The leaves of the plants were shiny—sticky-looking.

Later there started to be a great many white, new-looking fences and big white barns. The meadows around these barns, framed by the fences, were very green and smooth. On several of these places there were horses.

"Those are racehorses, aren't they?"

"That's right," Bert said.

"They look like any other horses to me."

Bert laughed. "What other kind of horses does a pool hustler see, anyway—except racehorses? . . ."

Downtown Lexington could have been downtown anywhere—all neon and glass and traffic. The hotel was called the Halcyon—there were others, but this was the one that Bert said had a poolroom in it—and they pulled up in front.

Eddie got out into the warm evening air, stretching his arms. "So this is Kentucky," he said, looking around.

"That's right," Bert said, walking into the hotel lobby. The lobby was big and elegant, and over on the far wall was a doorway and a sign above this saying, tastefully, BILLIARD ROOM. From this doorway, Eddie could hear the sounds that he always recognized—the crashing of balls and the soft murmur of men's voices.

"I'll pick up the reservations and get you a key," Bert said. "You can go ahead and check the battlefield, if you want."

"Thanks," Eddie said. He walked over to the door, carrying his little leather case.

17

HE COULD FEEL THE TENSION, the excitement of the place even before he opened the door, could hear the heavy undercurrent of voices, the clickings of many balls, the soft cursing and dry laughter, the banging of cue sticks on the floor. And when he went in he could almost smell the action and the money. He could even feel them, down to his shoes. It was like a whorehouse Saturday night and payday in the mines; the day the war was over and Christmas. He could feel his palms sweating for the weight of his cue.

Every table was going—two, four, even six-handed games. And on almost every table was a hustler. Near the front was the Whetstone Kid, short, red-headed, and wearing chartreuse slacks; Eddie had seen him play nine ball in Las Vegas. On the table behind him was another small man, an incredibly shabby person who specialized in shooting pool with drunks and in selling playing cards which, on their backs, illustrated the fifty-two classic positions in three colors. This fellow was known as Johnny Jumbo; Eddie had seen him in Oakland. In the middle of the room, surrounded by a small crowd of miscellaneous jockeys and tout types, Fred Marcum from New Orleans, a man with patent-leather hair and olive eyes, was talking with quiet agitation to a man whom Eddie knew only as Frank, and who was supposed to be the acknowledged master at jack-up pool, a seldom-played game. And there were others; he could tell by the styles of playing, by the feel of the games, even though he did not know the players, that there must have been dozens of them.

It was a panorama, a gallery. Bert had said that they followed the races; but Eddie had expected nothing like this, this convocation of the faithful, this meeting of the clans.

The room was packed with people. There were a few lost innocents: college boys with sweaters, and on one table a few men who could only be salesmen. These were playing a silly and awkward game of rotation pool, laughing uproariously whenever one of them miscued or knocked one of the balls off the table or shot at the wrong ball by mistake.

Eddie walked on into the room, was greeted by Fred Marcum and the Whetstone Kid, saw a few men glance at him furtively—and this made him feel very good and important—and found himself a place to stand over by the wall, where he could watch several games at once. . . .

After a few hours, after the crowd had thinned down somewhat—although the air was still full of smoke and money—Bert came in. He was still neat, but his hair was slightly mussed, and his trousers horizontally creased. He came making his way through the room purposefully—a stern broker walking smugly across the floor of the exchange.

Eddie looked at him. "Where've you been?"

"Watching a card game."

"Were you in it?"

"Not yet. It won't get worthwhile until later, anyway. But it should be a good one. There's some big men in it."

"There's some big men here too." Eddie nodded toward the poolroom in general.

"I know."

"Is it like this here all the time? Is this what they do in Kentucky?"

Bert smiled thinly. "No. I never saw it this way before. These boys follow the races, like I said; but I never saw this many pool players before. Or poker, either. It's like a convention." He looked at Eddie. "How're they doing? How's the money moving?"

Eddie grinned down at him. "The money's moving fast."

Bert pursed his lips, thoughtfully, pleased. "That's nice," he said.

"So what do we do?"

"Well, first," Bert said, slowly, like a woman about to decide on a hat, "first I put you in a game of pool. A medium-to-small game. Then I'm going back and see what's happening with the card game."

"Okay," Eddie said, and then, "What about Findlay—the man we came to see?"

"He'll be here. Maybe later tonight. Maybe tomorrow."

"Maybe we should go out to his house. You know where it is."

Bert shook his head. "No. That's not the way to play it. Findlay's not the kind you go ringing his doorbell and asking please can you shoot a little pool. He'll be around—just wait. You'll find enough to do while you're waiting."

Eddie laughed. "Okay, boss. Pick me a game."

"That's what I just been doing. See the jockey on the back table, practicing? His name's Barney Pierce."

"I see him. He doesn't look very good." The jockey was an immaculately dressed and loud-talking little man. He shot nervously and too fast.

"Well, he's better than he looks. He plays nine ball, and you ought to be able to beat him if you work at it."

"Okay," Eddie said. "Fine. But one thing."

"Yes?"

"I'd like to play him on my own money. I need the profit."

Bert started to answer and then did not. He thought a moment, chewing softly at his underlip, and then said, "All right. But don't pull that on me when I put you up against Findlay."

"I won't."

"Go ahead then. He probably won't go over twenty a game, in any case. You can start him at five."

"Thanks," Eddie said, walking over toward the end table, carrying his leather case. . . .

The jockey was considerably better than he looked, and as Bert had said he would not go past twenty a game. He knew more about nine ball than Eddie did, knew some very nice, safe shots that Eddie had never seen before, and he was very good at cutting balls thin; but Eddie beat him by shooting straight, concentrating on what he was doing and playing carefully. He was able to win more than a hundred dollars before the little man quit, slammed his cue into the rack, and departed. Eddie had started off in Lexington with a victory, a small one, and he liked the feel of it. Also, he liked the feel of money in his pocket, although that was not the important thing, not yet.

It was eleven o'clock when they finished and although there was still action in the poolroom it was too late to try for a new game. Bert was not around; there would be no telling when the poker game would be over.

Restless, he left the poolroom and began walking. It had been raining and the streets were wet and the air cool, clean and moist. There were not many people out—a few drunks, some newsboys, a cop. The city seemed pleasanter at night than it had when they had first driven in, shortly after supper. He continued walking, looking abstractedly into store windows, his hands in his pockets. Through his mind were circulating, slightly out of focus, images of Sarah, of Findlay—he had already formulated a hypothetical picture of Findlay, although Bert had never described him—and of Minnesota Fats. Somehow none of these people were very important at this moment, and he found himself mulling them over with detachment. It all seemed to have become very simple, walking here, alone, through a clean-washed and new town at midnight; what had been problems did not seem to be problems anymore. Findlay would be easy; he would win a good deal of money from him and that would be that. And Sarah was not really a problem. He did not owe Sarah anything. He would not even go back to

Sarah's when he got back to Chicago; she had nothing more to offer him, nor he her.

It began to drizzle slightly, and the sprinkling of rain that fell was surprisingly cold. Eddie ducked his head down and walked fast until he found an open café.

Inside he got coffee and scrambled eggs and listened idly to the juke box while he ate. The eggs were better than Sarah would have cooked them, and he caught himself grinning wryly at the thought of Sarah's poorly cooked eggs. He looked at his watch. A quarter of twelve. He would probably be having coffee with her now, if he were home. *Home?* What in hell did that mean—he didn't have any home. Certainly not with Sarah. But the idea stayed with him for several minutes, the idea of a house somewhere and Sarah, doing whatever women are supposed to do in houses. Him, reading the paper, buying a new car every year. Children—a back yard. At first it was amusing, but after a few minutes thinking it became unpleasant. He had lived in a home for too many years, with his parents, and he did not want any part of it. It had occurred to him once before that the whole institution—marriage, the home, the paycheck—was something invented by women, something they grew fat on at men's expense. What had Bert said—about wanting glory? Maybe that was right, maybe that was what was wrong with the house and the paycheck and the cute wife. Maybe that was why the married men all talked about the war they had once been lucky enough to be near to, while the women could make a whole, stupid life out of the new kitchen and what the baby was doing. He thought of his father, the tired and confused old man who had never quite made it. There were two things his father could talk about with love: what he had done during the first war, and what he was going to do when he got money. The poor bastard was probably right about the war, but he had never done anything about the money. Eddie had not seen him in four years, but he was probably running the same beat-up electrical shop, the We-Fix-It, in Oakland, and still wishing for a new car or a house or whatever tired old men wish for—maybe just a good lay.

He grinned to himself again—he could use a good lay himself. Then, struck by an unpleasant thought, he asked the man behind the counter, "What time do the liquor stores close?"

"In ten minutes, mister. Twelve o'clock even."

He paid his check quickly and left. For some reason which he did not fully understand he felt that it was very necessary to buy a bottle. He found a store in time and got a fifth of bourbon, which cost him forty cents more than the same brand in Chicago. It was Kentucky bourbon, and the label said, "Made in Bardstown, Kentucky." It didn't figure; but the types of hustle used in business seldom did, since the ways of the dollar were always devious. Or maybe it was taxes.

Bert had given him a key to the hotel room, which he had not been in yet. Still restless, he walked the four floors to the room and, bottle under his arm, unlocked the door.

The room was the living room of a suite; that was immediately obvious from the long and elegant gold couch, the big, soft armchairs, the little bar in the corner, and the door leading into the bedroom.

On the couch were two girls, both overdressed, both drinking.

He stopped in the doorway, holding the cue case, bottle and dangling key, thinking that maybe he had opened the wrong door, entered the wrong room. But one of the girls, the taller one, a blonde, said, giggling slightly, "You must be Eddie."

He paused. "That's right," he said. Then he walked in, set his things down in an empty chair, and began looking around the room. Inside now, he could see that there were two bedrooms. The living room was very big and expensive-looking. The carpet underfoot was thick.

"My name's Georgine," the blonde said. "Have a seat."

"Have a drink," said the other. She had brown hair and was prettier than the blonde.

"She's Carol," the blonde said. "Carol, meet Eddie."

"Hi," Carol said, smiling. Her teeth were somewhat uneven and she wore too much lipstick, but she was pretty.

"Hello," Eddie said, sitting in one of the armchairs. He wondered if Carol's bosom were real. Probably not, but nice if it were. Also the blonde's—Georgine's. Georgine walked to the bar and began pouring him a drink. She was wearing a black silky dress and it seemed that her butt might split it at any moment, but it did not. Her shoulders, he noticed, were round and very smooth, with a nice color to them. He wondered if they painted or powdered their shoulders, or if that was the way they looked naturally.

The blonde gave him the drink and then went back to the couch to sit down. She put a cigarette in her mouth, and when Eddie made no move to light it for her, shrugged her shoulders and lit it herself, with a match.

Eddie tasted his drink, which was strong. Then he leaned back and said, "You girls welcome all strangers in town this way?" He was watching the blonde's bosom as he said this, speculatively.

The brunette seemed to think this remark was very funny. When she had stopped laughing she said, "We're friends of Bert's. Didn't he tell you we were coming up? I mean, he told us you were coming." She seemed to think this was funny too.

"Somehow, honey," he said, "I didn't get the word. But now I've got it I'm glad to hear it." He was not certain how he felt about all this, and with Bert it didn't figure. Anyway it was interesting enough.

"I'm supposed to be your date," the blonde said.

"I'm glad to hear that too," he said. It occurred to him that the blonde had already drunk too much.

After a few minutes Carol turned the radio on and got dance music and when he finished his drink Georgine fixed him another.

And then Bert came in, looking very neat and collected but his face slightly flushed. "Hello, Georgine," he said, "Carol." Then to Eddie, "How'd you come out?"

"Fair. You were right about him. How did you make out?"

"All right." He took off his glasses and began wiping them with his handkerchief. "Fix me a drink, Carol, will you?" Eddie noticed an unfamiliar looseness in his voice. Then Bert smiled at him. "As a matter of fact I did very well. The game's still going on."

Then, when the girl brought Bert his drink he did a surprising thing. An amazing thing. He pulled the girl down beside him gently, took her chin in one hand and said, "Honey, you look great tonight." Then he laughed. Eddie had never heard Bert laugh like that, and he found it shocking.

Eddie watched him while he finished his drink. Then Bert

set his glass down, stood up, and began dancing with Carol. He danced too precisely, but well.

"Come on, Eddie, live it up," he said.

For Christ's sake, Eddie thought. Then he laughed himself. "Okay, Bert," he said. "You're the boss."

Georgine had come to sit by him on the arm of the chair. "You wanta dance?" she said.

"I'm a lousy dancer."

"That's the kind I like," she said. Then she pulled him up from the seat and he took hold of her and began moving around in approximate time to the music. She stood so close to him, however, that he could not do even that very well, and he finally stopped trying to move his feet and just held her and swayed. She seemed to go for this. She was all round protuberances, all of them very warm, all moving, and she rubbed against him a good deal. After a while this had the intended effect, and he was forced to sit down, pulling her into the seat beside him. He started to kiss her, and then stopped. Something was not right. "Get me a drink, will you?" he said.

"*Now?*"

"That's right. Now."

She got it and he drank it. Then he leaned around and kissed her.

Instantly her tongue was in his mouth, straining at his throat. And instantly he found his hand inside her dress. She smelled strongly of whiskey and of perfume.

She pulled back from him slightly. "You wanta go to bed now, honey?"

"What do you think?" He got up, taking her by the arm. Walking, he found, was difficult.

But in the bedroom she began doing something he did not like. She sat on the side of the bed and began methodically undressing, finishing her cigarette as she did so. She eased her stockings off quickly and neatly, set them beside the bed, then unzipped her dress. He did not like that. But he said nothing and just watched her. . . .

When they had finished he put his clothes on and went into the living room, which was empty. A hillbilly voice on the radio was pimping for a cut-rate jeweler's, "Just ninety steps from Main Street." The man sounded like a fool. The door to the other bedroom was closed. After he had mixed himself a drink and sat down he could hear them, Bert and the other girl. He could not imagine what Bert would look like in bed. Probably like everybody else looks, like some kind of awkward, sweating idiot. He wondered if Bert took his glasses off. Then he tried listening to the music, which had started again.

The blonde laid a hand in his lap, warm.

"No," he said.

"Later, maybe?" She was trying now to look at him lovingly. Apparently the pitch was that he had won her over by his little performance in bed. A commonplace hustle, probably always good for a second round. He wondered if Bert had paid them for the night, or only for each time; he did not know how such arrangements were made. This was a big-time arrangement: a hotel suite and two rented whores in party dresses. Or "call girls"—he had read that term somewhere, in a newspaper. The big-timers had call girls. You made a phone call and they came out. Very refined women. High-class. He looked at

Georgine for a minute, looked quizzically, drunkenly, at the smile she turned on immediately when she saw him watching her. Georgine was probably a call girl, the kind the newspapers wrote about. And here he was, Eddie Felson from Oakland, California, with this high-class, big-time whore, in a hotel suite in the middle of the horse-race country. Here he was, in Kentucky, hustling the hustlers, winning big money—Christ! He had hustled an old man, once, for a dime a game, back in Oakland, the year after he had quit high school. Now he was drinking expensive whiskey and having this expensive, high-class, big-time woman all for his own.

He looked at Georgine again and decided that he would have another drink. He needed one.

Bert seemed to take forever. Finally he came back into the room, his face red. He poured himself a small drink, looked at Eddie, pursed his lips thoughtfully, and then went to the bathroom where he began washing his hands and face.

Abruptly Eddie laughed, loosely. "Like Minnesota Fats?" he called at Bert. "Getting ready for the clutch?"

Bert came out of the bathroom, drying his face on a towel. "You might say that," he said, "but not," nodding toward the bedroom, "in that game."

"They say it's a good game."

"It's one of the best. But so is cards. And they're still playing upstairs." He began combing his hair, carefully.

Carol came out of the other bedroom barefoot. Her hair was mussed. She took Bert by the arm and said, "You're not leaving, honey? The night's young."

"That's right," Bert said, and then to Eddie, "and you better get some sleep. I got plans for you tomorrow."

"You had plans for me tonight," Eddie said, noticing with detachment that his voice was thick.

"All work and no play . . ." Bert said, leaving.

The girls went into the bathroom and began washing up and Eddie began working on another drink, although he felt that he shouldn't be drinking it. The lights in the room were too bright. He noticed that the fifth of bourbon he had bought was still sitting, unopened, in the chair. Like the fifth he had bought in Chicago more than a month ago. It had sat around for a week before he had given it to Sarah. But, then, that had been a fifth of Scotch. A high-class drink. And this was a bottle of bourbon. He stared at the bottle of bourbon for a long while, but made no move to get up from the couch and pick it up. He was still staring at it, drunkenly and stupidly, when the girls left and he told them tonelessly, good-by.

18

WHEN HE AWOKE THE NEXT MORNING, shortly before noon, his hands ached and there was a dull pain as though there were something alive and damp at the base of his brain. Walking into the bathroom he felt top-heavy and alone, and it was necessary to hold a cold washcloth at the back of his neck for some time before he felt that his blood was circulating again. Then he took a shower, tried to shake off some of the thickness in his head and to suppress the hard, aching feeling in his stomach, and then he woke Bert, who was in the other bedroom.

Bert woke easily but said nothing. Like Eddie he headed immediately for the bathroom, where he remained a long time. After he had dressed, Eddie came in to brush his teeth and found Bert sitting in the tub, a fleshy and solemn monarch, contemplating his genitals. Eddie began brushing his teeth.

"Good morning," Bert said.

Eddie spat mint foam into the basin. "Good morning yourself, sunshine."

"Feel better?"

"Better than what?"

"Better than yesterday."

"No. Worse. Why should I feel better?" He began rinsing his mouth out with cold water.

"No reason."

"That's a laugh." He hung up his toothbrush and turned to look at Bert again, who was now washing his pink arms, deliberately. "You always have a reason."

Bert tightened his lips in thought. Then he said, "I did, but I probably figured wrong. I figured your girl in Chicago was giving you a hard time, and that what you needed was what I hired for you last night."

Eddie stared at him. Then suddenly, he laughed, "For Christ's sake, you figure everything, don't you? Only this time you wasted your money."

Bert looked thoughtful, stepping out of the tub, dripping. "You *don't* have a girl in Chicago?"

"I did have. I don't know if I've got one now. Anyway, thanks, but Georgine didn't work."

Bert was drying himself and did not answer this. Then he went into the bedroom, sat on the bed, and started putting his socks on. Eddie began shining his shoes, still in the bedroom. Then Bert said, quietly, "You in love with that girl?"

Eddie stared at Bert for a moment, quietly. Then, suddenly, he began laughing. . . .

Waiting for the elevator he offered to split the cost of the room and the girls with Bert, now that he had more money, but Bert would not take it. He had played poker until four o'clock and had, apparently, won a good deal at it. Also, he said he figured to make his profit when they got the game going with Findlay. "Okay," Eddie said, "and thanks."

They ate a big meal in the hotel dining room and Eddie had two cups of strong coffee, which made him feel considerably better, although his hands were still stiff and sore. He did not say anything about his hands to Bert.

They went into the poolroom after eating and there were a good many people there for that time of day, although few were playing. In the back of the room was a group of five men who were obviously jockeys—little hard-looking men with lean faces and sharp eyes. There were several groups of other men in the room, most of whom Eddie did not recognize.

"Is Findlay here?" he asked Bert.

"No. I'll go ask about him." Bert walked over toward a group of three men who were standing by the cash register. One of them greeted him, "Hello, Lucky," to which he did not reply. It seemed a peculiar thing to call Bert. They began talking and Eddie could not hear what was being said.

He went over and took a seat near the jockeys, who were now being addressed by a thin man in a blue flannel jacket, whom Eddie did not recognize.

"Ignorance," the man was saying. "It's ignorance." Eddie did not attempt to follow the conversation, but it seemed that the man was trying to explain that atmospheric pressure was what kept pool balls on a pool table—without atmospheric pressure they would all fly off into space—and that, moreover, this phenomenon had a great deal to do with keeping horses on race tracks. The jockeys seemed skeptical, a feeling which Eddie shared.

After a while Bert returned and said, "Nobody's seen Findlay for a couple of days."

"Oh?"

"He might be at the races. You want to go out?"

"You're the boss."

"That's right," Bert said. "I'm the boss."

He had never been to a race track before—although, of course, he had bet the horses experimentally a few times—and at first it was quite interesting and exciting. There was the crowd, and the little windows, and the smell of horses, of women, and of money—most of all the money, which seemed to have a clean, outdoor smell to it, like a crap game in an open field.

But after the fifth race his feet were tired from the standing and he had become bored. He went into the bar, which was very horsy-looking and very crowded, and sat down. It was ten minutes before a waitress came, and during this time he looked at the people who filled the bar, most of them expensively, sportily dressed, and wondered where in hell they all came from and why, exactly, they were having such a good time. He could not fathom it. Gambling was something he felt that he understood, but to him gambling was betting on his own skill, or at least on an act in which he was personally involved, even matching quarters for drinks. This business of betting into rigged odds on somebody else's horse, which probably looked and behaved like any other horse anywhere, seemed to be a high kind of folly—or at least a simple amusement. But probably some people won at it, besides the track and the bookies. He had known a man who claimed to make a living betting horses. It did not seem to Eddie to be a decent way to make a living, even if the profits were high.

He amused himself for a while by trying to separate the people in the bar into two groups—the real and the phony rich. And there seemed to be a middle group: "Chamber of Commerce" or something, half real and half phony. You could tell by the clothes they wore. The rich ones usually wore ugly or grotesque clothes; the phonies were flashy, too stylish, and the Chamber of Commerce dressed very much the way Eddie did himself. The clothes of very rich people seemed to be almost invariably ugly, in the way that hand-painted ties are always uglier than factory-made ones, especially when worn with a pearl gray suit with whip stitching and a white-on-white shirt. And then there were the tweedy ones, but only a few. Almost all the women looked good, even the middle-aged women. Many of these were of the tightly packed, manicured, and overdressed sort whom Eddie had always found perversely attractive, but about whom he knew nothing, except that they liked to display it in public places, such as race tracks. For a moment he thought of Sarah's small breasts under her blouse, and he wondered what she would look like when she was forty. Probably tweedy and fat in the ass. Probably still living in an apartment and writing books. Maybe she would write one about him. A thin book, or a poem. Probably make her feel important, unusual, to be broad-assed and married to a college professor and to tell her friends about the pool hustler, the criminal, she had shacked up with once. But maybe that wasn't right. He did not have her figured out that well.

A waitress finally discovered him. He asked for a double Scotch, and watched her legs as she waded her way back to the bar. Standing at the bar was an interesting-looking man and Eddie shifted his attention to him while the waitress gave the bartender his order.

The man was tall and slim, with the kind of pale, debauched and oddly youthful face that some men of forty or more have. He was obviously rich and possibly a fairy, or maybe that was only the youthful, sensual look, for he did not seem effeminate. He was wearing a dark suit—Eddie could tell by the way it held to his narrow shoulders that it was very expensive—and dangling from his free hand was a very fine and expensive-looking camera. He was talking to a loudly rich type with binoculars, and both of them were laughing, only there was nothing humorous in the young-looking man's laugh.

The waitress returned eventually with Eddie's drink. It cost a dollar and a half, and she tried to hustle him out of a fifty-cent tip by fumbling the change and looking harried. He stoned her out on that one, however, waiting for his money.

She had just left when a bell rang loudly, signifying the end to betting for that race, and most of the people began to leave the bar or crowd to the windows, watching the track. But the man with the camera stayed at the bar, hardly aware, apparently, of the race that was starting.

Eddie listened for the sound of the bugle, then the noise of the horses running, which came a minute later, and with it the shouting and a few frenzied screams, the half-hourly orgasm. Then he finished his drink.

Bert came in, found him, and sat down.

Eddie stretched, and lit a cigarette. "How's it going?"

"Fair."

"You win on that one?"

"Yes."

Eddie shook his head. "You always win, don't you?"

Bert looked thoughtful. "As a general rule, yes." He glanced toward the bar. Immediately his eyebrows rose. "Well," he said, softly, "look who's coming!"

It was the thin man whom Eddie had been watching. He walked up to their table and sat down, lazily. Then he smiled at Bert. "Well, hello," he said, his voice soft, unctuous. "Haven't seen you in a long time."

"Hello," Bert said, pursing his lips in a faint smile. "I haven't been around here for a long time." And then, "I'd like you to meet Eddie Felson. James Findlay."

Eddie kept his face from showing anything. "Glad to meet you," he said.

"And I you." He set his camera on the table, and said, "I think I've heard about you, Mr. Felson. You play pocket billiards, don't you?"

Eddie grinned. "That's right," he said. "Here and there. Do you?"

"A little." He laughed. "Although I'm afraid I generally lose."

"So does Eddie," Bert said.

"Oh, I win sometimes," Eddie said, looking at Findlay. He noticed that the youthful look he had seen in the man's face was like a mask, or like the face of a middle-aged woman who is wearing too much make-up, as if something were holding the skin taut, preventing it from collapse, or from decay.

There was something supercilious, smug, in Findlay's voice, and in his almost blank, pale eyes. "I'll bet you do, Mr. Felson. I'll bet you do."

Eddie remained grinning. "How much?"

Findlay's eyebrows rose in mock astonishment. He turned to Bert. "Bert," he said, "I believe Mr. Felson is making a . . . proposition."

"That could be," Bert said.

Findlay looked back at him and smiled, and for a moment Eddie was amused at the situation—for it was obvious that Findlay knew the purpose of this visit, that Bert and Eddie would not be talking with him if there was not a hustle being planned. Findlay was playing it all out, and it occurred to Eddie that the man was an instinctive phony, a ham. "Well, Mr. Felson," he was saying, "maybe you would like to come out to my place some evening. We could play a few games of billiards."

Eddie did not like the word "billiards" when it was used to mean pool. But he smiled at the other man. "When?" he said.

Findlay smiled coldly. "You're very direct, Mr. Felson."

"That's right," Eddie said, grinning. "When?"

"Well," Findlay withdrew a cork-tipped cigarette from a black case and tapped it gently on the back of one hand. "Would you like to come out tonight? Eight o'clock?"

Eddie turned to Bert. "What do you think?"

Bert stood up, and then placed his chair back under the edge of the table. "We'll be there," he said. . . .

19

FINDLAY'S HOUSE ON THE OUTSIDE was like an Old Fitzgerald advertisement—the kind of a quasi-mansion that the word "aristocrat" means to some people. You had to drive a long way from the road before you could get to it, a big, dark brick box, with giant white columns in front supporting nothing, and shrubbery all over the place. By the black-top drive was a small, quaint metal statue of a Negro, in jockey uniform, holding out an iron ring toward a pair of white iron benches, fashioned to appear light and lacy and fooling no one, all very suggestive of the Old South, to which Kentucky had never belonged. The quaint metal statue was an ornament.

Inside, the place was more like an advertisement for Calvert's Reserve, the kind where a man who is graying at the temples sits in a leather chair and holds a glass of whiskey preparatory to swilling it. Going through toward the back, Eddie could see into a room filled with books and paintings, with several leather armchairs that would easily have made Findlay a man of distinction in any company. He began to wonder how his host would look bending over a pool table. It was an interesting thought.

The basement was veneered with mahogany on the walls, which struck Eddie as looking terrible, even worse than the shiny knotty pine that was the badge of something or other these days. In the back of the room was an ill-concealed furnace—it looked like a huge mahogany squid with metal arms—and next to this was a bar. In front of the bar sat the pool table, its green hidden by a gray dust cover. Over the table hung a row of shaded lamps, but these were not turned on yet.

They sat at the bar and Findlay fixed them all Scotches with soda. On Eddie's end of the bar was a wooden statue, about two feet high, of a man and woman engaged in one of the favorite indoor sports. Eddie looked at this with some interest, wondering briefly if it could really be accomplished that way. He decided that it would be possible, but fatiguing. Over the bar there hung a picture, also obscene, but not as imaginative. This was framed in white and appeared to be Japanese. The Scotch was very good, the best. Which figured.

Findlay had been keeping up a light patter of conversation, most of it aimless. He became quiet now, absorbed for the moment in his drink, and Eddie began to open his leather case. He took the cue out and screwed it together, checking it for tightness. Then he felt of the tip, which seemed to be a little too hard and slick, the leather battered down by innumerable tappings. He looked at Findlay. "You got any sandpaper? Or a file?"

Findlay smiled, almost eager to be of assistance. "Certainly. Which?"

"A file."

Obligingly, the other man went to a cabinet that was built into the wall, opened it, and withdrew a jointed cue of his own and a file, which he handed to Eddie.

Eddie took it and began carefully tapping the side of it against the tip of his cue, roughing it up a little to restore its springiness and to permit it to take chalk better. He glanced at his host, busily checking his own cue for tightness and straightness, sighting down it carefully. It seemed amusing, the two of them. Like a couple of gentlemen politely preparing their weapons for a duel. Which, in a sense, was what was happening.

When Findlay had finished performing his rites, Eddie said, "Let's play," and he stood up.

"By all means."

The minute they threw one corner of the dust cover back Eddie saw something that shook him. There were no pockets. It was a billiard table. He looked immediately at Bert. Bert had seen it too; he was pursing his lips.

Eddie looked at Findlay. "I thought you played pool."

Findlay raised his eyebrows with amusement. "I do. But not here, I'm afraid."

Eddie did not answer that but went on with him, folding up the cover and then putting it away on a shelf that had been built in for it, on the near wall. He weighed what was happening rapidly. He knew how to play billiards; and the game overlapped with pool anyway: both of them required a good stroke more than anything else, and a knowledge of what a ball would do. But the differences were great: the balls were slightly bigger and heavier; playing safe had an entirely different strategy to it; and most important, it was mainly a cue ball game—you did not concern yourself very much with where the ball you shot at went but with precisely what your cue ball did afterward. It was not easy for a pool player to get used to. And it was a tight game, a chesslike game, depending on brains and nerve and on knowing the tricks.

He looked at Findlay again. "What kind of billiards do you play?"

"Oh—three cushion?"

That sounded better. In three cushion there were some things that Eddie knew. And, in any event, it was not a runaway game; he could not get beaten without knowing what was happening to him. Unless Findlay was very damn good.

He looked at Bert. Bert was shaking his head "No."

Eddie grinned at him slightly and shrugged his shoulders.

Then he looked at Findlay and said, "And what do you figure is a good price for a game of three-cushion billiards? Say, twenty-five points?"

Findlay smiled, running his hand gently through his hair, which was thin. "A hundred dollars?"

Eddie looked at Bert. "How does that sound?"

Bert's face was tight. "Not very good. I don't think you ought to play."

"Why not?"

"What kind of billiard player are you? You probably never shot a game in your life."

"Oh, now," Findlay said, "I'm sure Mr. Felson knows what

he's doing, Bert. And certainly you can afford a hundred dollars to find out?"

"Sure he can," Eddie said. He began setting the white balls up for the lag and placing the red ball on the spot at the other end of the table. When he was through he looked over at Bert.

Bert's face showed nothing. Eddie chalked his cue tip.

"Well," he said to Findlay, "let's play."

They lagged for the break and Eddie lost, by a large margin. The balls seemed big and heavy, and he realized that they were made of ivory—bigger than the composition balls he was used to, and trickier to handle. They might be a problem at first; it would take a while to get used to them.

And the table—the table was too big. He had heard, somewhere, that they had used tables as long as sixteen feet, back when the game first was invented, in Europe. This one was a five by ten, but looking down it, it seemed to be at least sixteen feet. And the rails were strange, tight; and the cloth seemed different, a finer weave. He did not like it. When he shot into the white ball it felt big and heavy and seemed to resist the pushing of his cue, as though the bottom of the ball were sticking to the cloth.

Having won the lag, Findlay took the opening shot. His thin mouth frowning in elegant concentration, he stood, hands on hips, and sighted at the ball very carefully before he bent down to shoot. He made his bridge elaborately, letting the little finger on his left hand flutter several times before settling it down on the green. His preparatory strokes seemed to attempt gracefulness, but were merely wild swoopings for he held his cue too high at the butt and too far back, and the movement of his arm was irregular, jerky. But when he finally shot the cue ball, it hit the red ball, banked off the three proper rails, and hit the other white ball neatly. One point.

"Well," he said, smiling at Eddie, "that always feels pleasant, doesn't it?"

Eddie did not answer.

And Findlay made the next one, an easy three-rail air shot—the kind where the cue ball is sent for the three required bounces off the cushions before hitting the other two balls. He shot the same way, with the fluttering little finger, the swooping stroke, the phony frown of concentration. It was disgusting to watch his mannerisms. But he made two billiards.

When Eddie shot, he tried to play calmly, dispassionately, and he succeeded in making a good, smooth stroke and giving the cue ball a clean hit and roll. But he missed.

Findlay made another on his next turn, and then played him safe, by leaving Eddie's white ball at one end of the table and the other two balls at the other end. This, immediately, was a new problem; Eddie did not know exactly how to play safe from that position, and, irritated, he shot a wild shot which missed by several feet. The cue ball came *thunking* out of one of the corners and dropped dead in position for a simple three-rail cross shot for Findlay.

They continued playing and after a while Eddie began to make an occasional billiard. But he could not seem to get hold of the balls properly, could not get the feel of the table and of the game; and Findlay beat him. Twenty-five to eleven. When the game was over Bert handed Findlay a hundred-dollar bill, wordlessly.

"Thank you, Bert," he said, and then smiled at Eddie, the same supercilious, irritating smile. "Play another?"

He tried to concentrate on the simple shots during the next game, avoiding the tricky English—the kinds of spin that added extra variables to the way the ball would roll and bounce—and trying to cinch whatever shots he found. He lost, but he scored fifteen before Findlay beat him. He was not saying anything, was trying to keep himself from becoming angry with the silly, foppish way that Findlay played, trying to concentrate on winning—just winning. And every shot he played he could feel Bert's eyes, spectacled and quietly disapproving, watching him, his stroke, and the way that the balls rolled. But he did not look at Bert any more; he watched what he was doing.

And in the fourth game he finally began to get the sense of the balls and the table—the old, fine sense that always came to him, sooner or later, and let him know that it was going to be time for him to start to win. He began to loosen up, to put a little more wrist action into his stroke—although it hurt his wrist to do this—and he won the game, by a close score.

He won the next one, and then Findlay stepped behind the mahogany bar and fixed them drinks, strong drinks, and Eddie began to feel better, looser. It was time to bear down now, time to begin thinking of profits. And the game of billiards seemed to open up for him; the balls began to respond to his touch; and he began to enjoy the game, watching the balls fly around the table, enjoying the pretty little *click* at the end of each successful shot.

He won four out of the next six games and they were even again. He looked at his watch. A quarter to ten. The evening was just beginning; and, at last, he was feeling good, back in his element again. Now Findlay's exaggerated style of playing seemed only amusing, an opportunity for easy contempt.

After Eddie had won the game that put them even in money, Findlay went behind the bar to mix the drinks, and Eddie walked over to Bert and said, quietly, "When do I raise the bet?"

Bert considered this for a moment. "I don't know," he said.

Findlay was clicking ice behind the bar.

"I think I've got him," Eddie said.

"You're not supposed to be thinking."

"All right, boss." He grinned at Bert, amused. "I *know* I've got him, then. I'll beat him from here."

Bert looked at him carefully. "I'll let you know," he said.

But after the next game, which Eddie won, it was Findlay, surprisingly, who brought it up. He held his lighter out for Eddie's cigarette, and then, after clicking it dramatically shut, said, "Like to raise the stakes, Mr. Felson?"

Eddie looked at him for a moment, and then turned to Bert, "Okay?"

Bert's voice was noncommittal. "Do you think you'll beat him?"

"Of course," Findlay said, smiling. "Of course he thinks he can beat me, Bert. He wouldn't be playing me if he didn't. Right, Felson?"

"It figures," Eddie said, smiling back at him.

"I didn't ask him *can* he beat you," Bert said. "I already know he can beat you. What I asked him was *will* he. With Eddie that's two different things."

Eddie looked at Bert for a moment, silently. Then he said, his voice level, "I'll beat him."

Bert pursed his lips, unimpressed. "We'll see." And then, to Findlay, "How much?"

"Oh . . ." Findlay scratched his chin, delicately. "What about five hundred?"

Instantly, Eddie felt a small tightening in his stomach, not unpleasant. They would be getting down to business now.

"All right," Bert said.

Eddie, looking at Findlay's hands, noticed that the nails seemed to be polished. Even after playing pool they were impeccably clean, perfectly trimmed, and slightly glossy.

Findlay beat him. The score was close, and Findlay did not seem to shoot any better, nor Eddie any worse; but Findlay made more billiards than he did. It cost Bert five hundred dollars, and Bert paid it silently.

Eddie lost the next game the same way. Findlay's playing was still as affected, as silly looking, as ever; but he won.

And it was during that game that a very revealing shot came up, one that changed for him the whole aspect of the game. It was Findlay's shot, and the balls were spread in a very tricky position. There was what appeared to be a simple, easy setup; but actually the balls were arranged so that a last-minute kiss—a collision between the two wrong balls—would have been inevitable. A poor player would not have seen this, a player as poor as Findlay seemed to be.

But Findlay did not shoot the shot in the obvious, predictable way. He put a great deal of reverse English on the cue ball, skidded it into the side rail, across the table twice, and into the middle of the third ball. The shot did not look like very much; but Eddie immediately recognized it for what it was, and the recognition was a pronounced shock. It had been a professional shot, the shot of a man who knew the game of billiards very well.

"Well," Eddie said quietly, "maybe I ought to sign you up."

Findlay laughed softly, but did not say anything.

Eddie began watching him closely, and began to notice some things about his stroke. It seemed jerky and awkward, but on the shots that counted there was a slight smoothness that was not there on the others.

It was hard to take, hard for Eddie to swallow: he was being hustled.

After the game Findlay offered to fix them another drink; but Eddie said, "I think I'll sit this one out." He walked over to the bar beside Findlay, though, and leaned on it casually and watched while he fixed his drink. Something was going on in his mind, obscurely. Then, when Findlay was stirring the drink, he looked at him closely, looking at his eyes, and said, "You play a lot of billiards, Mr. Findlay?"

And when Findlay said, "Oh . . . every now and then," in his supercilious voice, Eddie saw in his face what he had been hoping he would see. He saw self-consciousness and deceit. And over it all the general sense of weakness, of decay.

But he did not beat Findlay the next game. He started with confidence of his superiority, with calm confidence; but he lost. And the next one. This made him two thousand dollars—of Bert's money—behind.

He had not spoken to Bert for several games. After losing the last one, he watched Findlay go behind the bar again and then he turned to Bert and said, "I'll get him this time."

Bert looked at him coldly. "How are the hands?"

He had not been thinking about them, and he became abruptly aware that they were hurting him severely.

"Not too good," he said to Bert.

Bert kept looking at him; and then he laughed, softly. But he did not say anything.

And Eddie felt himself suddenly reddening. "Now wait a minute. . . ."

"Shut up," Bert said. "We're leaving."

For a moment Eddie's head spun. Then he said, "All right. All right," and turned back toward the table, beginning to unscrew the cue, to separate the two pieces.

And then he stopped. This was not right.

He turned to Bert, and looked at him. "No," he said. "We're not leaving. You've got me figured wrong this time. I can beat him."

Bert did not say anything.

"I'm going to beat him. He fooled me. He fooled me bad because he knows how to hustle and I didn't think he did. He probably fooled you, too, if that's possible—for anybody to fool you. But I can outplay him, and I'll beat him." And then, "He's a loser, Bert."

Bert's voice was level, but it had no edge to it. "I don't believe you."

Suddenly, Eddie turned away from him, looking at the bar and at the fat obscene wooden figures on the bar. "All right," he said. "Go home. I'll play him on my own money." Then he said loudly, to Findlay, "Where's your toilet?"

Findlay inclined his head toward the stairway. "Upstairs, Mr. Felson. To your right."

Eddie walked up the stairway, his feet heavy and lifeless under him, and into the huge, high-ceilinged parlor, now empty. He walked through it, on thick and silent carpet, and to the bathroom, from which a light shone.

The room was a small, old one, with lavender-striped paper on the walls. He walked to the toilet and seated himself on the edge of it carefully and for several minutes thought of nothing. Then he filled the lavatory bowl with hot water, took soap and a towel and began washing his face and hands, scrubbing at the creases in his face, getting the greenish dirt off his wrists. There was a brush sitting on the edge of the bowl and he cleaned his fingernails with this. Then he refilled the bowl with cold water and rinsed his face, hands, and wrists. There was a comb in his pocket and he used it to comb his hair, neatly and carefully. He rinsed his mouth with water from the tap, spitting it out into the bowl.

Then he sat down again and began bending his thumbs, slightly at first and then more. They hurt; but they did not hurt very much; not as much as he remembered them hurting a few minutes before. They did not hurt so much that he could not stand the pain, not at all. *That's one excuse,* he said, softly. Then he forced himself to think of the times he had played three-cushion billiards before; there had been a great many times, over a period of many years. And Findlay was not very good. That was the other excuse. He got up and looked at himself in the mirror. His face was clear, youthful. *And I'm not drunk.* And then, still looking at himself, he said aloud, levelly, "You're going to beat that son of a bitch downstairs. That's because you're Eddie Felson, one of the best." Then he went out and back down to the basement.

When he came back into the room he felt clean, clear in the head. And he felt something else, very slight, a small almost undetectable sensation, a thin, nervous, taut sense. Of power.

Findlay was standing by the bar, elegantly slim, a drink in

his hand; and his face, lit by the brilliant lamps over the pool table, looked as if it might crack at any moment, as if the thin smile on his lips would shatter first and then a long, jagged crack might appear under his eyes, spreading downward until pieces of face, like plaster, would chip and fall to the floor. And Bert still was sitting in his chair, solidly planted, like a wise vegetable, keeping his own council.

Eddie walked to the table and picked up his cue, holding it for a moment and looking carefully, with pleasure, at the polished shaft, the silken-wrapped butt, the white ivory point and the little blue leather tip. All of this time a small voice in him was saying, *You've got five hundred and forty dollars. What if you lose the first game?* But he did not listen to the voice, since there was no point in listening.

He looked over at Findlay, and then at the picture, the picture of a man and two women, pink and naked, on grass, over Findlay's head; and then he grinned at Findlay. "Let's play," he said.

Findlay took the opening shot and made it, but missed the next one. Eddie stepped up to the table, bent down, sighted carefully, stroked, and made a billiard. Then he made another; and another. Then he played safe.

Before he shot, Findlay said dryly, "It looks as if you mean business this time."

"That's right," Eddie said.

When Findlay shot, he did not take quite as much care with the elaborate procedure, although he still rippled the little finger as he made his preliminary strokes. But he made a billiard, and then another. He missed the third by less than an inch.

It looked as if he meant business, too, and Eddie thought with exultation, *This is the clutch. I was right.* And he stroked with care. He made one billiard, but he missed the next, by a heart-breaking, last-minute kiss.

They played it safely and with great attention to detail, and Eddie played the best game of three-cushion billiards he had ever played in his life. But when it was over, Findlay had won. He had won by only two points, but when Eddie handed him the five hundred dollars he had to look at him and say, "That's all of it. I'm broke."

Findlay's eyebrows rose gently, and Eddie could have kicked him in the stomach for the gesture. "Oh," he said, taking the bills and smoothing them out with his fingers, "That's unfortunate, Mr. Felson."

Eddie looked at him coldly. "Who for, Mr. Findlay?" He began unscrewing his cue.

Then Bert, who was sitting behind him, said, "Go ahead and play him, Eddie. For a thousand a game."

Eddie turned slowly, looking at Bert's face, searching, for a moment, for a trace of a smile. There was no smile, nothing. "What brought you to life?" he said.

Bert pursed his lips, looked at Findlay, looked back at Eddie. "I think maybe the odds have changed," he said.

"What am I—a race horse?"

"In a sense, yes."

"Well, now," Findlay said, "it seems as if you might know something, Bert. You're making me think I should be careful."

"A raise in the bet usually has that effect," Bert said.

"And you know something?"

Then Bert smiled, very slightly. "It's like in poker, Mr. Findlay. You're going to have to pay to find out."

Findlay stared at him a moment and then made a gesture with his hand. "Perhaps I won't have to pay at all, Bert," he said. "Perhaps I know something too."

Bert was still smiling. It was exactly as if he were sitting behind a large, round table, holding five pasteboard cards in his small, pudgy hand.

"Let's find out," he said.

Eddie was still looking at Bert and, for a moment, he felt as if he would like to pat him on the back, buy him a drink, or something.

And then Findlay was saying, "All right, Bert, we'll find out. For a thousand a game." He finished his drink and set it down, carefully, on the edge of the bar, next to the piece of sculpture.

Then Findlay pointed a thin finger at the belly of the man in the little group of intertangled people—a little, paunchy belly with a deeply carved navel that caught the bright light from over the pool table—and said, "Have you noticed, Bert—this fellow here bears a striking resemblance to you. It seems almost as if you might have modeled for the artist."

Bert pursed his lips. "It's possible," he said.

For the first time that day, Eddie laughed. He laughed loudly and long. Then he said, "You're a comedian, Bert. A real comedian."

Findlay stared at him amusedly while he laughed. When Eddie had finished he said, "Let's play billiards, Mr. Felson."

From the first shot Eddie knew he had him. The three balls were standing out on the green now like jewels—machined, honed and polished gems, and the feel of the balls had come to him completely. And the long table—he liked the long table now, liked the long rolls of the heavy balls, the inexorable way that he could make them roll, ponderously, down the table and across, banking off the rails and into other balls. It was a fine game, a sedate, chesslike game, and he saw it now for what it was, a game that he could understand and control and that he would, eventually, win at.

He won. And he won the next game. And, after that one, a very close and tense game, he began to hear the little reasonable voice that said, *You can ease up now, it isn't that important,* and he forced the voice to shut up. And doing this, forcing himself to bear down even harder, to concentrate even more, it began to be clear to him that what Bert had said about character was only a part of the truth. There was another thing that Bert had only partly seen, had only partly communicated to him, and this was the fixed, unvarying knowledge of the purpose of the game—to win. To beat the other man. To beat him as utterly, as completely as possible: this was the deep and abiding meaning of the game of pool. And, it seemed to Eddie in that minute of thought, it was the meaning of more than the game of pool, more than the five-by-ten-foot microcosm of ambition and desire. It seemed to him as if all men must know this because it is in every meeting and every act, in the whole gigantic hustle of men's lives.

The squirrel's voice, the voice of his own cautious, uncommitted ego, had told him that it wasn't important. He looked at Findlay, at the vain and sensual face, the sly, homosexual eyes; and it seemed astonishing to him now that he had not seen how necessary it was to beat this man. For it *was* important. It was very important.

It was important who won and who did not win. Always. Everywhere. To everybody . . .

After Eddie had won the third game, the third thousand-dollar game, he began to see a strange and wonderful thing: Findlay started to crumble.

He began to drink more and sit down more between shots, and when he got up to shoot there was a kind of haughty weariness in his movements. Occasionally he laughed, wryly—Sarah's kind of laugh—and Eddie could hear in Findlay's laugh the words, almost as if they were spoken to him, *It doesn't make any difference. It doesn't make any difference because, no matter who wins, I'm better than he is.* And Eddie knew that he was seeing now what Minnesota Fats had seen when he himself had fallen apart under pressure and self-love. It was a fascinating, a disgusting, frightening, and contemptible thing to watch. And Findlay did not quit, and Eddie knew now that it was because there was no way for him to quit, that he was being drugged, was drugging himself into playing, game after game, as if something were going to happen, as if it were going to turn out that, somehow, it was all untrue, and that he, Findlay, had somehow come out of it all serene and happy and important.

Findlay crumbled, fled, fell, oozed, and became disjointed; he became petty, vain, and ridiculous; but he did not quit for a long time. When he did quit it was almost nine o'clock in the morning and he had lost a little more than twelve thousand dollars.

Leading them upstairs, he smiled wanly at them, and said, "It's been an interesting evening." He looked very old, especially in the face.

Eddie looked at him for a moment, intently; and it seemed that there was something pathetic and yet eager in the faint smile on Findlay's thin and now almost bloodless lips. Then he looked away. "It sure has," he said.

They left the house then, walking out, shockingly, into sunlight and the smell of wet grass. . . .

Before Bert started the car he counted off for Eddie his share of the money—three thousand dollars. The bills were beautiful with the old magical color; and Eddie, whose senses still seemed so acute that there was nothing that could not be seen by him, responded with sensitivity and depth to the fine, impeccable lines of engraving, the sharpness of detail, and the excellent, tasteful numbers in the corners of the bills. Then he put the money in his pocket.

Outside the window, in Findlay's drive, the air was clear and cool, with a faint mist. The sun was bright, but low. There were birds, discordant, adding to the sense of unreality. Eddie could see orange and yellow tinges on the leaves of trees, and could feel an edge in the air. Summer was ending. It was a fine and strange morning, full of imminent meaning.

He looked at Bert and said, "Well?" And it occurred to him then, looking at Bert, that there was nothing more for Bert to teach him; that he had learned, in this game that his hands and arms in their soreness were still remembering, a lesson and a meaning of his own, and that there was nothing more to do with Bert except to cut loose from him, to become free of him.

And when Bert did not reply, Eddie said, pushing him, "You think I'm ready now for Fats?"

"What about the thumbs?"

"The thumbs are all right."

They were on the road that led to town, and Bert drove them in silence for several minutes before he answered. "If you're not ready now you never will be."

Eddie lit a cigarette, cupping his hands against the wind. His body seemed to feel tense and relaxed at the same time, but the sun on him was warm, pleasant. "I'm ready," he said.

20

FOR THE FIRST THREE HOURS OF THE TRIP north Eddie did not say anything. They were in Ohio by mid-morning. Traffic was very light. It was very strange to be riding in this big car in the autumnal morning, his body dimly aching from the long night's work, his eyes grainy and yet alert, and to be driving toward Chicago. Two months before he had driven to Chicago, with Charlie Fenniger. That seemed now to have been a long time ago. What would Charlie be doing now? Opening the poolroom in Oakland, brushing the tables? Charlie had been his friend for a long time. Once, years before, he had admired Charlie, had thought Charlie was a first-rate pool player.

And Bert, what about Bert? Bert, like Charlie, was a teacher and a guide—a guide not to pool playing, but to gambling. Bert knew the wheels that turned in gambling and the wheels within the wheels. You could never really pin down a man like

Bert, get hold of him, find out exactly what his meaning was. But Bert was necessary, if only because of his intelligence and strength—as, in a different way, Sarah had once been necessary, during the time that his own world had been tilted and confused. Even Sarah—weak, losing Sarah with more of her twisted than just her leg—was a tremendously necessary person. Or *was* Sarah a loser, or only a person who was not in the game because she did not understand the rules? But who knew the rules? Bert, if anyone.

But there was the rule—possibly the only real rule—that he had had to learn himself, the rule that Bert had not actually told him, the one that had come to him with such clarity when he had been playing Findlay, the rule that was a command: *Win.* And yet maybe that was what Bert meant by character—the need for winning. To love the game itself is a fine thing; it is loving the art you live by. There are many things to love in the art—the excitement of it, the difficulty, the use of skill—but to work at it only for those would be to be like Findlay. To play pool you had to want to win and to want this without excuses and without self-deception. Only then did you have a right to love the game itself. And this reached further. It seemed to Eddie now, sitting in Bert's car, his body sore and his mind tremendously aware, that the need to win was everywhere in life, in every act, in every conversation, in every encounter between people. And the idea had become for him a kind of touchstone—or a key to the meaning of experience in the world.

But as he became gradually more tired, more hypnotized by the steady movement of the sunlit road before them, the awareness and the insight began to fade, leaving, as these things always do, a few new ideas, or prejudices. And, possibly, a little more knowledge of what his own life was about. . . .

After a while he dozed for a few minutes, and then wanted to talk. There was something he had wanted to ask Bert. . . .

"Say," he said, his voice drowsy now, "where does Fats get his bankroll?"

For a while he thought that Bert was not going to answer him at all, and he was about to ask the question again when Bert spoke. "I saw him beat a whorehouse operator named Tivey out of thirty-six thousand dollars. Tivey had heard about Fats and wanted to try him at one-pocket. That was about eight months ago." Bert looked thoughtful. "He makes a mark like that once a year or so. There's always somebody who likes to gamble with the best. And then," Eddie could see him grin slightly, "there's always people like you. What did he take from you?"

"About six thousand."

"I didn't think it was that much."

"Maybe it wasn't. My partner was holding it." And then, "What do you think Fats makes a year?"

"Hard to tell," Bert said. "One thing you probably don't know about him, he hustles at bridge too. And he owns property. I went in with him myself once on a piece of property, a Chinese restaurant, and we did all right." Bert was silent for a minute, driving, his eyes straight ahead. "Fats is smart. He gets along."

"Like you?"

"Maybe." And then, pursing his lips and looking straight

ahead, "He does better than I do. I think maybe he's got something I don't have."

"What's that?"

Bert seemed to be concentrating with tremendous attention on his driving, although there was no one else on the road. Then he said, "Fats is a very talented man. He always was."

For quite a long time, Eddie did not say anything. They stopped and bought sandwiches and beer and then, back in the car, Bert said, "Why all the questions about Fats? You thinking of replacing him?"

Eddie grinned faintly, "Not replacing, exactly. More like joining his club."

"It's a hard club to join. There aren't fifty top pool hustlers in the country who make a living at it."

Fifty sounded like a small number, but it sounded right. "Maybe," Eddie said. And then, "We'll see."

When they were coming into Chicago Bert said, "Where do I let you out?" It was three o'clock in the afternoon.

After trying to think for a minute, Eddie said, "Where do you stay?"

"At home. On Sullivan Avenue."

Struck by the word "home," Eddie stared at him. "Are you married?"

"Twelve years." Bert adjusted his glasses with one hand, the other on the wheel. "Two girls in school."

"For Christ's sake!" Eddie said. And then, "Let me off at a hotel. Any hotel, maybe near the Loop somewhere."

The hotel was in a part of town he was unfamiliar with. When he got out of the car he stopped and said, "You coming up to Bennington's tomorrow?"

"What time?"

"I don't know. After lunch, I think."

"Okay," Bert said. "I'll meet you here for lunch at two. Then we'll go see George together."

"George?"

"That's right. George Hegerman. Minnesota Fats."

"Well, what do you know?" Eddie said. "George Hegerman." And then, "All right. I'll see you at two." He took his suitcase and his little round satchel and went into the hotel.

Normally this kind of thing could provide him with a good feeling, walking into a hotel lobby with three thousand dollars in his pocket. But he felt slightly uneasy, and he could not help wondering whether Sarah would be waiting for him.

After he had checked in and had unpacked he did not know what to do. He took a shower, and immediately was surprised to find how good that could make him feel—hot water, soap, and then cold water. It was so pleasant that he decided to shave. He did so, stung his face with shaving lotion, brushed his teeth, cleaned his fingernails, polished his shoes, put on clean underwear, and then began scuffling in his bag for a clean shirt and slacks. There weren't any, and he was forced to put on the ones he had been wearing. Then it occurred to him that he could buy some new clothes, that, in fact, he ought to. This was a very pleasant idea, and he left the hotel and found a clothing store.

He bought carefully, enjoying it. He liked the power over all of the rows of suits, racks of ties, the fine wool, silk and cotton, that having a great deal of money gave him. He bought a dark gray suit, single-breasted and narrow at the shoulders, a pair of gray slacks, and a pair of tan ones. Then he bought a half-dozen shirts, another half-dozen socks, underwear and, finally, two pairs of shoes. Everything was of the best quality. When he was finished, the clerk was beaming and Eddie was beginning to feel a thing that he deserved to feel, after the strange and very satisfactory week in Kentucky. It was a kind of nirvana—like the sensation produced by a long drink of whiskey in the morning, before lunch. But, unlike whiskey, the feeling did not bode a dissolution into seediness and malaise; but, rather, a general tapering off into quiet pleasantness which, tomorrow, would be followed by something better, but of a different kind. There were pleasure and life in all of this; and they had come upon him unexpectedly, after taking a shower and while buying expensive clothes at suppertime.

It came to almost three hundred dollars; and he gave the man an extra five, telling him to have the pants cut to length for him right away. The man said it would take a half hour.

Eddie left the other things at the store and began walking around in the neighborhood, looking into store windows idly, amazed at how fine he was feeling and how pleased.

Then he came to a jewelry store and there were wedding rings and engagement rings in the window. He looked at these for several minutes, almost hypnotized by the way the gems flashed in the bluish light from the display lamps. You could buy a very fine-looking ring for two hundred dollars. Somehow, he had thought they cost more than that. Two hundred dollars, now, did not seem like very much money at all.

A strange thing about this line of thinking was that he did not really think of Sarah at all, nor did he think about the absurdity of offering her a ring, or of what, conceivably, he could say, holding out one of those little velvet boxes that rings come in and saying, “Let’s get married,” or whatever it is you say at such times. He just stood, looking at the rings. Then he walked into the store.

But, in spite of his peculiar condition of mind, Eddie was not a stupid man. He bought a two-hundred-dollar lady’s wrist watch and had it wrapped in a small white box.

The clothes were ready and he took them back to the hotel. He almost took another shower before he got dressed but settled with washing his face again, and then looking in the mirror. He looked good; his eyes and skin were clear, his hair glossy. When he put on the fine, clean, new-smelling clothes he felt as if he could sing. What was happening to him? He felt lovely, fine, as if the act of dressing in a new suit were a baptism and an orgasm, as if he were putting on wings. He had played pool all night the night before, with Findlay, and had slept lightly on the long car ride. His body was tired—he could feel the tiredness underneath the vigor that was infusing itself in him—but he felt more alive and aware, more perceptive and happy than he could remember ever feeling in his life. When he was dressed he threw the old clothes away, stuffing the wrinkled shirt and pants into the wastebasket.

Then he went out, carrying the little white box with the watch in his pocket. He hailed a cab and gave the driver Sarah’s address.

And suddenly, walking up the steps to Sarah's apartment, he became nervous. The door to the place was closed. He hesitated a moment, and then knocked.

And then the door was open and she was looking up at him. She was holding a book in one hand, the other on the doorknob. Her hair was neat around the sides of her face; she was wearing her glasses. She had on a new blouse, a dark one, tucked in neatly at the waist.

"Hello, Eddie," she said, quietly. Then she stepped back from the door. "Come in."

The apartment was clean, cleaner than he had ever seen it. Even the clown's frame had been dusted off! and there were no scattered books or glasses. He took a seat on the couch and looked around him. He looked at her; but she was not looking at him.

Then, still not looking at his face, she said, "Can I fix you a drink?"

"Sure," he said. "Thanks."

When she was in the kitchen, opening the ice tray, she said, "How was Lexington?"

"Fine," he said. "Better than I expected."

She walked in and handed him the drink, then turned away. "That's nice," she said. She sat down in the easy chair, across the room from him.

He still felt very good. The room was cool, his body and clothes were very clean, and he let the whiskey send its warm hands rubbing comfortably against the lining of his empty stomach.

He had anticipated her coolness, and was amused by it. But there seemed to be nothing to say. When he had finished his drink he stood up. "You eaten dinner yet?"

She glanced at him momentarily. "No," she said. "I haven't."

"You want to go out? To the place we went last time?"

She drew in her breath. "I don't know."

"Please."

"That's an odd word for you to say."

"That's right. Do you want me to say it again?"

She stood up. "You won't have to." She set her drink, unfinished, on the coffee table. Then she walked into her bedroom, shutting the door behind her. "I'll be out in a few minutes."

She was through in fifteen minutes. The outfit did not look as good as it had the first time, because she had not dressed as carefully. But she looked very nice, high-class. He thought of the whore in Lexington. When they left he started to take her arm gently in his hand, but thought better of it.

She nursed only one martini before dinner, and did not finish that one. Nor did she talk very much.

He had two highballs, with bourbon, and after the second one began to regain his sense of pleasure, which had been showing symptoms of waning, but the pleasure was different now—strained, and not so intense. "How's school?" he said.

"School is over. Until September."

They both ate the roast beef, which was rare and very good. They went through the rest of the meal silently, and when it was over he gave her a cigarette and lit it for her before he spoke. "I bought you something."

She smiled faintly, but said nothing.

He took the little package from his coat pocket and handed it to her.

She took it, glanced at it, and then looked up at him, quizzically. "Is this an apology, maybe?"

"I don't know. Maybe."

She opened the box and took the watch out into her hand. It was a plain silver watch, with a thin black strap. He had picked it because it had the feel of class to it. She looked at it carefully for a moment, then put it on her wrist. "It's lovely," she said.

He took a drink from his coffee cup. "I almost bought you a ring."

Abruptly she took her eyes from the watch and stared at him, closely. Her eyes were wide. Finally she said, slowly, "What kind of a ring?"

"What kind do you think?"

She was still watching his face, her eyes penetrating and puzzled. "Are you telling me the truth?" she said, "Or are you . . . hustling?"

"With me that's sometimes the same thing." He lighted a cigarette. "But I'm not lying to you. I almost bought a ring."

"All right. Then why didn't you buy it?"

He was not certain why, so he did not attempt to answer her. Instead he said, "Suppose I had?"

She looked down at the watch. "I don't know. Maybe you did the right thing." Then she smiled, and the puzzled look disappeared from her eyes. "Anyway it's a fine watch. I'm glad you gave it to me."

He looked at her for a minute, her face, neck, and shoulders. She seemed very young. Then he stood up. "I'll take you home."

They walked silently, and he listened to the odd rhythm of her heels, the uneven cadence that the limp made. They passed the bus station, and he started to say something but did not. He held her arm, crossing the streets, and he felt excitement at it, the soft bare arm, warm and smooth in his hand. But she did not look up at him, nor did she respond to his pressure. He felt now as if something were wrong; and he did not know what to do. The drinks were wearing away, and the work of the last several days was beginning to catch up with him. It seemed to be a very long walk.

Climbing the stairs to her apartment was very difficult. His feet were burning and there was lead in his shoulders and, when he got to the top, there was vertigo. He realized, abruptly, that it had been a long time since he had rested. Somewhere, his sense of pleasure had dribbled away. Suddenly, he wanted very much to go back to the hotel and sleep for a very long time, to stretch out and become unconscious. A bed in a quiet room would be very fine. His head was aching.

She opened the door, but instead of going into the room stood in the open doorway, looking at him. Then she said, slowly, "If you want a drink you'll have to get a bottle, Eddie." Her voice was tired, but not unpleasant. "I only have a little left on hand."

"Tuesday was the first of the month," he said. It occurred to him that neither of them had acknowledged the fact that he had not brought his suitcase with him.

"I got my check," she smiled faintly, wryly. "I had to use the liquor money for tuition. The fall semester." She looked away from him, inspecting the doorknob it seemed. "You can get a bottle of Scotch if you'd like, and we can drink it."

"In Coca-Cola glasses?"

She did not look up. "If you want to."

He was looking at her face, fascinated by her skin, which seemed to glow in the soft light from the living room lamp. But he felt nothing, only a simple, admiring fascination, as if he were looking at the orange clown on Sarah's wall, the one in the white frame. The clown that had once seemed ready to tell him something. "You didn't finish your martini tonight," he said.

"I know."

"Maybe it's a good sign," he said gently, feeling almost as if it were someone else talking to her, as if he himself were already at the hotel, in bed, alone. "You don't make a very convincing lush."

"No," she said, looking up at him now. "I don't suppose I do." And then, "Are you going to get the Scotch?"

"No," he said. "I'm tired. And I have a big day tomorrow."

"Are you coming in? There's a little left in my bottle."

He looked at her face, the wise and hard and puzzled eyes. "I'd better be getting back to the hotel," he said.

She looked at his eyes, for the first time that night. She did not seem to be trying to find anything in them, just looking. Then she said, "Thanks again for the watch."

"I'm glad you like it." He turned and began walking down the stairs.

"Good luck, Eddie," she said, calling softly to him, "for tomorrow."

"Thanks," he said. He continued down the steps slowly to the landing, listening for the final sound of her door closing. He heard nothing. Then, at the landing, he turned and looked back up. Sarah was still standing there, looking at him. The light was from the open doorway behind her and he could not see her face. "Sarah," he said, his voice soft, strange, "I came very close to buying that ring. . . ."

She did not reply, and he stood there, looking at her, for what seemed a very long while; but he could not make out her features. Then he turned and continued down the stairs.

He took a cab to his hotel, since he did not feel like walking. When he went to bed he did not fall immediately asleep.

21

BENNINGTON'S HAD NOT CHANGED. It was not the kind of place that would change. It was two o'clock in the afternoon when Eddie and Bert stepped from the elevator, walked across the hall and through the huge door. Inside, the room was very quiet. No one was playing pool and there was virtually no one in the place, except for a small crowd of eight or ten men sitting and standing against one wall.

Most of the men seemed familiar to Eddie. One of them, a very big, meaty-looking man with glasses, Eddie recognized as the poolroom manager, Gordon. He did not know any of the others by name, except for one of them. In the middle of the group, sitting, speaking to no one, was Minnesota Fats. He was cleaning his fingernails, with a nail file.

Gordon had looked up when Eddie and Bert walked in, and in a moment they had all stopped talking. Eddie could hear a radio playing, faintly, but nothing else. He looked at

Fats. Fats did not look up. There was a very strange sensation in Eddie's stomach; he would not have known what to call it. A polished voice on the radio announced something and then music began to play—a love song.

Bert kept walking and found himself a seat at the edge of the group. Several of the men nodded to him and he nodded back, but no one said anything.

Eddie had stopped beside a table in the middle of the room; he stayed there and began opening his leather case, carefully. While he was doing this he watched Minnesota Fats, not taking his eyes from the moonlike face, the shiny, curly hair, and the massive belly, now covered with tight blue silk—a pale blue shirt that fit so tight across Fats' belly that it clung to it, folding only where the flesh folded, under the narrow belt. On his small feet, Fats was wearing immaculate little brown-and-white shoes, which rested delicately against the foot rail of the chair that held his magnificent, enormous butt.

While Eddie watched him, taking his cue stick from the case and then twisting the two ends together, Fats' face made its regular, jerking grimace, but his eyes did not look up at Eddie.

Then Fats finished what he was doing, slipped the nail file into his breast pocket, and blinked at him. "Hello, Fast Eddie," he said, in the no-tone voice.

The stick was together now, and tight. Eddie walked to Bert, handed him the case, and then, cue in hand, he walked over to Fats, stopping in front of him.

"Well, Fats," he said, "I came to play."

Fats' face made the heavy, ambiguous movement that resembled a smile. "That's good," he said.

Not saying anything, Eddie turned around and began racking the balls on the empty table in front of the sitting men. When he had finished he began chalking his cue quietly and said, "Straight pool, Fats? Two hundred a game?"

From somewhere in the heavy mound of silk- and leather-wrapped flesh in the chair came a kind of short, softly explosive sound, a brief travesty of a laugh. And then, blinking, Fats said, "One thousand, Fast Eddie. One thousand dollars a game."

It figured. It figured immediately; but it was a shock. Fats knew him now. Fats knew his game, and Fats was not going to fool with him, was going to try to put him down fast, on nerve and on capital. It was a good move.

Not answering, Eddie bent down and began tapping the cue ball with his cue stick, gently shooting it across the table and back. He kept his hands busy with the cue stick, to keep the fingers from trembling. He kept shooting the cue ball, back and forth across the table, and he thought of the two-and-a-half thousand dollars in his pocket, the dim pain in the fingers of his hands, the stiffness in the joints of his thumbs and in his wrists. And he thought about the money and nerve and experience and skill backing the grotesque and massive man who was sitting behind him now, jerking his chin, watching.

If he played him, he would be bucking the odds. Immediately he thought of Bert again. Bert would never buck the odds. Suddenly he looked up and over at Bert. Bert sat, squat and secure, looking down at him from the high chair, his face clouded, his eyes registering disapproval. No, Bert would never buck the odds.

Eddie stood up from the table and, not looking at anyone, said, "Flip the coin, Fats. Let's see who breaks. . . ."

Fats broke, and he was beautiful. His stroke was lovely; his command of the game miraculous; and the graceful movements of his giant, disgusting body were a compound of impossibility and of genius. He beat Eddie. Fats beat him not just once, but three times in a row.

The scores were close, but it happened so fast that Eddie felt he did not have any control of what happened. Balls had bounced and slipped and rolled and fallen into pockets, and, as before, Fats had seemed to be everywhere, shooting fast, never looking, playing his obscure concerto with his fiddlebow of a cue and his musician's hands with emeralds on the fingers.

For the last twenty minutes of the final game Eddie did nothing but watch while Fats edged and sliced and nursed and coaxed balls to perform for him, making a run of ninety-three and out. When he gave him the thousand, the last thousand, Eddie's hands were sweating and he was still staring fixedly at the table. There was a ringing sound somewhere in his head. Then, still hardly aware of what had happened to him, he looked up.

He was in the middle of a crowd. People were sitting all around the table, all of them watching him. Nobody else was playing pool. It was late afternoon now. There was slanting autumn sunlight in the big room, and everything was very quiet, except for the radio, which seemed to be tinkling and buzzing.

He could not distinguish individual faces in the crowd very well at first, but they began to come into focus. He was looking for Bert; he did not know exactly why. He should not want to see Bert, but he was looking for him. And then he saw Charlie.

He blinked. It was Charlie, no one else, sitting in a chair by the wall, pudgy, bald at the temples, and with no expression on his face. He started to walk to Charlie, to ask him where he had appeared from, what he was doing there; but he stopped, struck in the face by an insight.

Charlie had come to smirk at him, to see him beaten again. Charlie, like Bert, one of the in-turned and self-controlled—one of the cautious, smirking men. Maybe Fats was like that too, maybe the three of them were brothers under the pink flesh, delighting quietly in the downfall of the fast and loose man, finding the weak spot—suddenly it seemed to Eddie that he himself was a Lazarus of sore, weak spots—and then, having found the place where it hurts, gently probing and pushing and twisting until their mutual enemy, the man with all the talent, was lying on the floor vomiting on himself.

Looking at Charlie he could see himself now as a man crucified, and Charlie as his Judas. He could have wept, and he made fists out of his hands and tightened them until he felt that he would scream with the pain. And then the edge of his vision caught sight of Bert, and immediately he came to his senses and saw what he was doing, playing the loser's game with himself, the game of self-pity, the favorite of all the multitude of indoor sports. . . .

Charlie eased himself up from the chair and waddled over. His face was serious, his voice quiet. "Hello, Eddie," he said. "I just got word you were playing up here."

"Why aren't you in Oakland?"

Charlie attempted a smile. The attempt was a failure. "I was. Last week I started getting worried about you and flew back. I been hunting you. Around the rooms."

"What for?" Eddie stared at him; there was something

strained about the way Charlie was talking to him. "What do you want me for?"

Not answering at first, Charlie fumbled in his hip pocket and withdrew what looked like a folded-over checkbook and held it out to him. "This is yours," he said.

Eddie took the book and opened it. It was full of traveler's checks, in denominations of two hundred fifty each. "What the hell . . . ?" he said.

Charlie's voice was back to its customary lack of expression, like that of a comic miniature of Minnesota Fats. "When you were drunk up here before and hit me for the money, I held out on you. This is what I held out. A little under five thousand." And then, abruptly, his face broke into one of his extremely rare smiles, which lasted only for a moment, "Minus my ten per cent, of course."

Eddie shook his head, letting his thumb run over the thick edges of the blue checks. It figured; it figured, but it was hard to believe: he had just come back from the grave. "So why give it to me now," he said. "So you can watch me lose?"

Charlie's voice was soft. "No," he said. "I been thinking. Maybe you're ready to beat him now. Maybe you were ready before—I don't know. Anyway, you ought to find out."

"Okay," Eddie said. He grinned at Charlie, the old grin, the charm grin, fast and loose. "We'll find out."

He glanced at Fats, who seemed only to be waiting, and then counted the money. There was four thousand five hundred in traveler's checks, and he had about seven hundred in cash. His whole kitty. *Well, here we go. Fast and loose.*

Then he looked at the fat man and said, "Fats," thinking, *you fat bastard,* "let's play a game of pool for five thousand dollars."

Fats blinked at him. His chins jerked, but he said nothing.

"Come on, Fats," he said, "five thousand. That's a hustler's game of pool. It's my whole bankroll, my life's savings." He flipped again through the book of checks, not feeling the pain that doing this caused, and then looked for a moment at Charlie. Charlie's face showed nothing, but his eyes were alert, interested, and Eddie thought, wonderingly, *he's going along with it.* Then he looked at Bert and Bert was smiling thinly, but approvingly; and this, too, was astonishing and lovely.

"What's the matter, Fats?" he said. "All you got to do is win one game and I'm gone back to California. Just one game. You just beat me three."

Fats blinked at him, his face now very thoughtful, controlled, and his eyes as always a kind of obscene mystery.

"Okay," he said.

Having changed the bet they tossed for the break again, and Fats lost again. He chalked his cue carefully, stepped sideways up to the table, set his hands on the green, the rings flashing, and shot.

The break was good, but not perfect. One ball, the five ball, was left a few inches out from the rack, unprotected, down at the foot of the table. The cue ball was frozen to the end rail, the table's length from it. It was an odds-off shot, a nowhere shot; and Eddie's first reaction was automatic, play it safe, don't take a chance on leaving the other man in a place where he can score a hundred points. The proper thing to do would be to ease the cue ball down the table, nudge one of the corner balls, and return it to the end rail, letting the other man figure it out from there. That would be the right way to play it—the safe way.

But Eddie stopped before getting ready to shoot and looked at the ball and it occurred to him that although it was a very difficult shot it happened to be one that he could make. You cut it just so, at just such speed and with just so much spin and the ball would fall in the pocket. And the cue ball would split open the rack and the ball game would suddenly be wide open.

It would be smarter to play safe. But to play safe would be to play Bert's game, to play Fats' game, to play the quiet, careful percentage. But, as Bert himself had once said, "There's a lot of percentage players find out they got to work for a living."

He chalked his cue lightly, with three deft strokes. Then he said, "Five ball in the corner," bent down, took careful, dead aim, and shot.

And the cue ball—for a moment an extension of his own will and consciousness—sped quickly down the table and clipped the edge of the five ball, then rebounded off the bottom rail and smacked firmly into the triangle of balls, spreading them softly apart. And while this was happening, the little orange ball with the number 5 in its center rolled evenly across the table, along the rail, and into the corner pocket, hitting the bottom with a sound that was exquisite.

The balls were spread prettily, the cue ball in their center, and Eddie looked at this loose and lovely table before he shot and thought of how pleasant it was going to be to shoot them into the pockets.

And it was a pleasure. He felt as if he had the cue ball on strings and it was his own little white marionette, darting here and there on the green baize as he instructed it by the gentle prodding of his cue. Watching the white ball perform, watching it nudge balls in, ease balls in, slap balls in, and hearing the soft, dark sounds the balls made as they fell into the deep leather pockets gave him a voluptuous, sensitive pleasure. And in operating the white marionette, putting it through its delicate paces, he was aware of a sense of power and strength that was building in him and then resonating, like a drumbeat. He pocketed a rack of balls without missing, and then another and another, and more, until he had lost count.

And then, when he had finished cleaning off the table and was standing, waiting for the rack man to put the fourteen balls back together in their triangle, he realized that the balls should be already racked but they were not, and an absurd idea struck him: he might have already won the game. Fats might never have had a shot.

He looked over to the chair where Bert was sitting. Fats was standing there, beside Bert. He was counting out money—a great many hundred-dollar bills. Fats seemed to be taking an impossible amount of money from his billfold. Eddie looked at Bert's face and Bert peered back at him, through the glasses. Someone in the crowd of people coughed, and the coughing sounded very loud in the room.

Fats walked over and set the money on the edge of the table, his rings flashing under the overhead lights. Then he walked to a chair and sat down, ponderously. His chin jerked down into his collar for a moment, and then he said, "It's your money, Fast Eddie." He was sweating.

He had run the game. He had made a hundred twenty-five balls without missing, and had shot in nine racks of fourteen balls each, making and breaking on the fifteenth ball each time.

Eddie walked to the money, the silent, bulky money. Instinctively, he wiped some of the dust from his hand on the side of his trousers before handling it. Then he took it, rolled up the green paper, pushed it down into his pocket. He looked at Fats. "I was lucky," he said.

Fats' chins dipped quickly. "Maybe," he said. And then, to the rack boy, "Rack the balls."

Out of the next four games Eddie won three, losing the one only when Fats, in a sudden show of brilliance, managed to score a magnificent ninety-ball run—a tricky, contrived run, a run that displayed wit and nerve—and caught Eddie with less than sixty points on the string. But Fats did not sustain this peak; he seemed to fight his way to it by an effort of will and to fall back from it afterward, so that his next game had even less strength than before.

And Fats' one victory did not affect Eddie, for Eddie was in a place now where he could not be affected, where he felt that nothing Fats could do could touch him. Not Eddie Felson, fast and loose—and, now, smart, critical, and rich. Eddie Felson, with the ball bearings in his elbow, with eyes for the green and the colored balls, for the shiny balls, the purple, orange, blue, and red, the stripes and solids, with geometrical rolls and falling, lovely spinning, with whiffs and clicks and tap-tap-taps, with scrapings of chalk, and the fingers embracing the polished shaft, the fingers on felt, the ever and always ready arena, the long, bright rectangle. The rectangle of lovely, mystical green, the color of money.

And then when Eddie had won a game and was lighting his cigarette Fats spoke out grimly with words that Eddie could feel in his stomach. "I'm quitting you, Fast Eddie," he said, "I can't beat you."

Eddie looked across the table at him, and at the large crowd of men behind him. There stood Minnesota Fats, George Hegerman, an impossibly big man, an effeminate, graceful man. One of the best pool players in the country, George Hegerman.

Then Fats came around the table, ponderously, gave Eddie fifty one-hundred-dollar bills—new ones, fresh from the bank—took his cue down to the front of the room, and placed it carefully in its green metal locker. He turned and looked back at Bert, not looking at Eddie. "You got yourself a pool player, Bert." Under the armpits of his shirt were large dark stains, from sweat. For an instant, his eyes shifted to Eddie's face, contemptuously. Then he turned and left.

Men began to get up from their seats and stretch, began to talk, dissipating for themselves the tension that had been in the room for hours. Eddie's ears were buzzing, and his right arm and shoulder, although they were throbbing dimly, felt lightweight, buoyant. Vaguely, he wondered what Fats had meant, speaking to Bert. He turned and looked at Bert, smiling to himself, his ears still buzzing, his hand still holding the thick sheaf of new, green money.

And Bert sat small and tight. Bert the mentor, the guide in the wilderness, with the face smug and prissy, the glasses rimless, the hands soft and sure and smart—Bert. Bert, with the gambler's eyes, reserved, almost blank, but missing nothing.

Bennington's was almost empty already. It must have been very late. Eddie rolled the sheaf of bills into a fat cylinder and pushed this carefully down into his pocket, still looking at Bert. Out of the corner of his eye he could see Charlie, still sitting;

and down at the front of the room Big John, the man with the cigar, was taking a cue stick out of the rack and inspecting its leather tip, thoughtfully. Behind Bert, Gordon, the big man with the glasses, the man who was always in Bennington's, was still sitting, his hands folded in his lap.

Eddie grinned at Bert, tiredly. He felt very happy. "Let's get a drink," he said. "I'm buying."

Bert pursed his lips. "I'll buy," he said, and then, "with the money you owe me."

Eddie blinked. "What money?"

Bert peered at him a moment before he answered. "Thirty per cent." He smiled tightly, thin-lipped. "It comes to forty-five hundred dollars."

Eddie was staring at him now, the grin frozen on his face. Then he said, softly, "What kind of a goddamn joke is that?"

"No joke." What had been barely a smile left Bert's face. "I'm your manager, Eddie."

"Since when?"

Bert seemed to be peering at him with great intensity, although it was impossible to tell exactly how his eyes looked behind the heavy glasses. "Since I first adopted you, two months ago, at Wilson's. Since I started backing you with my money, since I taught you how to hustle pool."

Eddie drew a breath, sharply. After letting it out, he said, his voice level, cold, "You little pink-assed son of a bitch. You never taught me a goddamn thing about hustling pool."

Bert pursed his lips. "Except how to win," he said.

Eddie stared at him, and then, suddenly, laughed. "That, you son of a bitch, is a matter of opinion." He turned away and began unscrewing his cue, holding the butt of it tight to keep his fingers from trembling. "It's also a matter of opinion whether I owe you a nickel."

Bert did not answer for a minute, and when Eddie had finished with the cue and turned around he saw that Gordon was now standing by Bert's chair, his arms together behind his back, looking at Eddie and smiling slightly, like a sporting goods salesman.

"Maybe," Bert said. "But if you don't pay me, Gordon is going to break your thumbs again. And your fingers. And, if I want him to, your right arm. In three or four places."

For a moment, he was hardly aware of what he was doing. He had, instinctively, backed up against the pool table, and he was gripping the weighted, silk-wrapped butt of his cue stick in his right hand.

Bert was still peering at him. "Eddie," he said quietly, "if you lay a hand on me you're dead." Gordon had his huge, meaty hands at his sides now, and was standing slightly forward of Bert's chair. Eddie did not move; but he did not release his grip on the cue. He looked around, quickly. Charlie still sat impassively. Big John, heeding nothing, was practicing now on the front table, shooting a red ball up and down by the rail. Over the big door was the clock. It said one thirty-five. He looked down at the cue butt in his hand.

"You'll never make it, Eddie," Bert said. "And Gordon's not the only one. We've got more; and if Gordon doesn't, one of them will."

Eddie stared at him, his head a buzzing confusion. "*We?*" he said. "*We?*" And then, suddenly, he began laughing. He let the cue butt fall on the table, and gripped the rails, trembling, with his hands, and laughed. Then he said, his voice sounding strange and dim to him, "What is this? Like in the movies? The Syndicate, Bert—the Organization?" The buzzing seemed finally to be leaving his ears and his vision was clearing, losing its fuzziness. "Is that what you are, Bert: the Syndicate Man, like in the movies?"

Bert took a minute to answer. Then he said, "I'm a businessman, Eddie."

It did not seem real. It was some kind of melodramatic dream, or a television show, or an elaborate game, an indoor sport....

And then Bert said, his voice suddenly softening, as it sometimes could, after the clutch was over, "We're going to make a lot of money together, Eddie, from here on out. A lot of money."

Eddie said nothing, still leaning against the table, his body strangely relaxed now, his mind clear with dreamlike clarity.

And then Charlie said, "You better pay him, Eddie."

Eddie did not look at him, keeping his eyes on Gordon, especially on his hands. His voice was soft, controlled. "You're not in this, Charlie?"

Charlie did not answer for a minute. Then he said, "No, I'm out of it, all the way out. But they're in, and you're gonna have to pay."

Eddie let his eyes move from Gordon's hands to Bert's face. "Maybe," he said.

"No," Bert said. "Not maybe." He pursed his lips, and then adjusted his glasses with his hand. "But you don't have to pay it now. You can think about it for a couple of days."

Eddie was still leaning against the table. He lit a cigarette. "What if I leave town?" he said.

Bert adjusted his glasses again. "You might make it," he said. "If you stay out of the big towns. And never walk in a poolroom again."

"And if I do pay it?"

"Your next game will be about a week from now—with Jackie French. We've already talked to him about it, and he wants to try you. Then, next month or so, there'll be people coming in from out of town. We'll steer some of them to you."

Eddie felt very steady now, and the buzzing was completely gone from his ears, the trembling gone from his hands. "That's not worth thirty per cent, Bert," he said.

Bert glanced up at him quickly. "Who said it was? Who said it had to be?"

Eddie's voice was calm, deliberate. "Why don't you and Gordon go out and roll drunks, if you're in the muscle business?"

Bert laughed softly. "There's no money in rolling drunks. And just how pretty is the business you're in?" Then he stood up from his chair and bent, brushing the creases from his trousers. "Now let's go have that drink."

"You go ahead, Bert," Eddie said. Then he picked the pieces of his cue up from the table, and began putting them in their leather case. He looked up at Gordon. "You run this place, don't you, Gordon?" He snapped the lid of the case and tossed it to Gordon, who caught it silently. "Find me a locker to keep that in." Then, looking at Bert, he said, "You better go on home—to your wife and kids—Bert."

"Sure," Bert said, peering at him intently, his voice flat. "But remember, Eddie. You can't win them all."

Eddie looked at him and then grinned, very broadly and easily. "No," he said, "but neither can you, Bert."

Bert continued looking at him for a minute. Then, saying nothing, he turned and left, walking purposively and slowly past the big oaken door.

About twenty minutes after Eddie and Charlie had left, Henry, the colored janitor, began to cover the tables with their gray oilcloth covers. After he had done this he closed the windows and pulled the heavy draperies together over them, so that it was extremely still, tomblike, in the huge room. Then, before locking up, he stopped to watch Big John shoot his eternal practice shot one final time for the evening.

Big John, ready to leave, ready to return to his obscure bed in some unknown hotel, shot with firmness and resignation, his pink arm stroking quietly and surely. The tip of his cue struck the cue ball, the cue ball hit the three, and the three ball, red and silent, rolled up the green table, hit the cushion, rolled gently down, and into the corner pocket.

ALSO BY

WALTER TEVIS

THE QUEEN'S GAMBIT

Eight-year-old orphan Beth Harmon is quiet, sullen, and by all appearances unremarkable. That is, until she plays her first game of chess. Her senses grow sharper, her thinking clearer, and for the first time in her life she feels herself fully in control. By the age of sixteen, she's competing in the U.S. Open Championship. But as Beth hones her skills on the professional circuit, the stakes get higher, her isolation grows more frightening, and the thought of escape becomes all the more tempting.

Fiction

THE COLOR OF MONEY

Twenty years have passed since "Fast" Eddie Felson conquered the underground pool circuit. During that time he married and opened his own pool hall. But he's left that all behind and is now badly in need of money, and pool is all he knows. On the beautiful aquamarine waters of the Florida Keys, he ropes his former rival Minnesota Fats into a series of exhibition matches in the hopes of picking up a cable TV deal. But while playing the old master, a terrible feeling nags at him—that he's sat on his talent and the best part of him is now gone. When he vows to get back in the game—seriously this time—he finds a challenging road ahead, and the only thing standing in his way is himself.

Fiction

THE STEPS OF THE SUN

The year is 2063. Earth's energy resources are dangerously close to being depleted, a new world superpower has upset America's global dominance, and the threat of another ice age looms large. Fortunately, there is one man brave enough—and perhaps foolish enough—to venture beyond the planet to find the mineral resources that will secure the country's future: Ben Belson. One of the richest men in the world, Belson is haunted by personal demons and wanted for his unlawful space travel, but he will stop at nothing to fulfill his crucial mission—and discover a future greater than he could ever have imagined.

Fiction

MOCKINGBIRD

As Robert Spofforth ascends to the top of the crumbling Empire State Building, his only wish is to be able to step off the ledge. But as one of the last androids tasked with overseeing the bleak persistence of mankind, his programming prevents him from ending his long and tired life. In this world where reading has been forgotten, physical contact is forbidden, and the vestiges of humanity idle away their days in a narcotic haze, the future is decidedly grim. But when Paul Bentley, an unremarkable man who makes a remarkable discovery, shares his new knowledge—called reading—with an unusual woman named Mary Lou, the order of their desolate world is challenged and a new hope for humanity glimmers amid the ruins.

Fiction